NORSE MYTHS AND LEGENDS

NORSE MYTHS AND LEGENDS

TALES AND SAGAS OF THE GODS & HEROES

SIRIUS

SIRIUS

This edition published in 2024 by Sirius Publishing, a division of
Arcturus Publishing Limited,
26/27 Bickels Yard, 151–153 Bermondsey Street,
London SE1 3HA

ISBN: 978-1-3988-4440-7
AD012240UK

Printed in China

CONTENTS

INTRODUCTION

Emilie Kip Baker (1873–1951) was married to Franklin T. Baker, founder of the Department of the Teaching of English at Columbia Teachers College. She published a number of volumes of re-told myths and legends with the aim of making the stories accessible to the widest audience but had an enjoyable but educational purpose at the heart of her storytelling. This collection of stories was first published as *Stories from Northern Myths* in 1914.

Norse mythology is the body of myths belonging to the peoples of northern Europe and more specifically Scandinavia. Many arose from Old Norse religion, but continued after the Scandinavia embraced Christianity, and fed into the Nordic folklore of the modern period. Norse myths are considered the northernmost extension of Germanic mythology, Norse mythology consists of tales of various deities, beings, and heroes. Derived from numerous sources from the pagan period and earlier, including medieval manuscripts, archaeological representations, and folk tradition, the source texts include deities such as Thor, the god of thunder, Odin, flanked by his ravens, the goddess Freyja, with her chariot drawn by cats, along with many other gods.

Much of the Norse mythology that survives, is based around the plight of the gods, along with and their relationships with

other beings, some of them humans as well the *jötnar*, beings who may be friends, lovers, foes, or family members of the gods. In Norse mythology a central sacred tree, Yggdrasil is the centre of the cosmos, surrounded by the "nine worlds". Certain units of time and elements of the cosmology are personified as deities or other beings. Most the Norse mythology we know today is drawn from two sources, the Eddas: two Icelandic literary works, a collection of poems and a prose work, both containing many stories; and the Sagas, prose stories and histories, originating in Iceland and elsewhere in Scandinavia.

The tales recounted here are drawn from both sources and contain most of the best known legends from Norse mythology including how Odin sought for wisdom, how Thor gained his hammer – and his many trials, the story of why the Fenris Wolf was bound, as well as, threaded through several of the stories, the activities of Loki, the trickster god, who eventually gets his comeuppance.

Thrilling and elemental, the stories reach right back to the very founding of the world and tell of lands of fire and ice and the gods and men who try to contain them.

1

HOW ALL THINGS BEGAN

Long, long ago, before the earth was made – and there was no sea and sky or night and day – the vast, unending Land of Mist stretched away on one side of a bottomless gulf, on the other side of which lay the Land of Fire. The Land of Mist was called Niflheim, and here eternal winter reigned with fog and snow and darkness that wrapped the dreary land about like a shroud. From the heart of Niflheim there flowed a dark, tumultuous river, and as it rushed down into the chasm at its edge, the waters met the cold blasts that swept up from below, and great mountains of ice were formed on the side of the gulf over which the chill fogs gathered and the bitter winds blew.

The never changing twilight which brooded over the gulf was sometimes illuminated by sparks that were blown over from the Land of Fire that lay just beyond. This place was called Muspelheim, and here the whole land glowed like a living furnace with flames that burned with the heat of a million suns. Sparks of

fire flew up in great numbers into the clouds, and these, glowing like balls of fire, were thrown far and wide on the land. Some of the burning sparks floated northward toward the land of snows, and as they fell into the ice-filled gulf, they changed to clouds of steam which were soon congealed into hoar-frost. Then one day this great mass of frost, on which fresh sparks of fire still fell, was suddenly warmed into life, and out of ice and snow and fire and heat the great giant Ymir was made.

Now although Ymir was fashioned out of these strange elements and so never felt the cold, he was soon very hungry in his home of ice and snow, and there was no food to be found anywhere. For a long time the giant wandered over the frost-bound land, and then one day he came upon the gigantic cow Audhumbla, who stood among the ice-hills calmly chewing her cud. From her udders flowed four streams of milk, and this was more than enough to satisfy the giant's hunger. He never strayed far from the wonderful cow, and one day, as he watched her licking salt from the blocks of ice, he was surprised to see a head suddenly appear through the melting ice. Audhumbla kept on licking with her strong, rough tongue, and soon the whole body of a man emerged. As this strange being stood before the eyes of the astonished Ymir, the giant was filled with fear and hatred, for he knew that from the mighty Iceman would spring a new race that would soon make war upon the giants and destroy them.

This is, indeed, just what did happen later on, for from the children of the Iceman came the gods Odin, Vile and Ve, who began at once to make war upon Ymir and all his kindred. In the terrible battle that took place between the gods and giants, Ymir was killed; and from his body poured forth such a great river of blood that all of the giants were drowned in it except two. These were Bergelemer and his wife, who escaped on a chest that floated away to the edge of the world. From them sprang a new race of frost-giants who continued to make trouble for the gods just as their forefathers had done.

Then Odin took the body of Ymir, and with the help of his brothers he fashioned from it the earth and the sea and the sky. From the great masses of flesh they formed the earth, and all around it they planted Ymir's eyebrows to make a high fence as a protection against the frost-giants. His immense bones they shaped into hills, and out of his teeth they made the cliffs, while his thick hair they used for trees and bushes and grass. His blood supplied the boundless ocean, and his skull formed the arching sky in which the gods placed some of the sparks that floated out of Muspelheim. These they caught and set in the heavens and called them stars. The sky was held in place by four strong dwarfs who stood east and west and south and north with the great weight resting on their shoulders. All this work seemed good in the eyes of the gods, and they knew that everything as it left their hands would prosper if only the frost-giants would stay in Jötunheim – their dreary, fog-wrapped country that lay beyond the ocean which now encircled the earth.

To the giantess Night, and her son, Day, the gods gave chariots and swift horses, so that they might drive through the sky every twenty-four hours. Night had a dark chariot drawn by the black

horse Hrimfaxe (Frosty-mane), who rushed so swiftly through the heavens that drops fell from his sweating flanks and bit, and these became dew or hoar-frost as they lighted on the earth. Day drove a white horse which was called Skinfaxe (Shining-mane); and when the chariot of his dusky mother sank out of sight behind the hills, he harnessed his shining steed and followed in the same path she had chosen.

Beside the chariots which belonged to Night and Day, the gods set two others in the heavens to light the newly made earth. From the flames that leaped forever out of the Land of Fire they made the sun and moon, and placed each one in a golden chariot so that they might be driven through the sky. The horses which drew the sun and moon were beautiful white creatures with shining golden manes. In order that the restive steeds of the sun should not be scorched by its fierce heat, the gods placed a great shield in front of the chariot to protect the animals' flowing manes. The moon horses did not need anything to stand between them and its mild rays.

Then Odin chose Mani and Sol – the son and daughter of a giantess – to drive the chariots of the sun and moon; and the story goes that many, many years later, when there were people on the earth, Mani looked out of his golden chariot one night and saw two little children – a boy and a girl – carrying between them a heavy pail of water. These children were the servants of a cruel giant who made them work all night instead of sleeping; and Mani, feeling very sorry for them, and being rather lonely all by himself, put out a long arm and caught up the children from the

earth. Then he set them beside him in the moon; and they have remained there with Mani ever since.

The frost-giants, who loved dreariness and gloom, were very angry when they saw how bright the world was with the light of the sun and moon; so they sent two fierce grey wolves to follow close upon the track of the bright chariots. Sometimes they came so near that their great black shadows dimmed the brightness of the sun, and sometimes they hung so close to the wheels of the moon-car that its light never reached the earth. The wolves never succeeded, however, in eating up the chariots, though their grim shapes often lingered threateningly in the sky.

When the gods had formed the earth – which they called Midgard – they chose the most beautiful spot they could find for their home. In the very centre of the earth rose a lofty mountain, and on the top of it was a broad, lovely meadow where the gods built their shining city of Asgard. In the midst of the city was a spacious hall, made of gold and the purest marble, and here were the thrones where the gods sat when in council. Beyond the hall were the palaces of the gods and goddesses, also made of marble and silver or gold, and nearby was a huge smithy where the gods forged the weapons needed to defend their city from their enemies the frost-giants.

From Asgard to Midgard the gods stretched a rainbow bridge which they called Bifrost; and over this they passed and repassed on their frequent journeys to the earth. There was no human being on the earth at this time, and the gods felt sorry that no eyes but their own could look upon the fruitful, blossoming land. No

one ploughed the fields or built houses, or sailed in ships across the seas. No voices of children rang over the meadows; no sound of the reaper's scythe broke the stillness of the fields; and no ringing of metal on the smith's firm anvil was heard throughout the silent earth.

Then the gods took some of the earth-mould and made of it a host of tiny creatures which they called Dwarfs or Gnomes; but when Odin saw how ugly they were, with their misshapen bodies and great heads, he condemned them to live underground and never to come up into the light of day. So the dwarfs spent their time delving into the heart of the earth for gold and silver and precious stones; and they became the cleverest workmen at their tiny forges, making wonderful things of every kind of metal. They were cunning, too, and kept their secrets well, so that neither gods nor men knew the hiding-place of their treasures.

Besides the dwarfs, the gods made the Fairies – or Elves – but these were so airily and daintily fashioned that they seemed to belong to the sky instead of the earth. So the gods built the fairy folk a home between Midgard and Asgard – a beautiful place called Elfland, all made of rainbow colours and moonbeams, and gossamer silks and delicate spiders' webs. The gods also gave these little people gauzy wings so that they could fly down to earth and play with the butterflies, and make caps of harebells, and dance in the moonlight round a fairy ring. They were never wicked and spiteful like the Gnomes, though they sometimes liked to play good-natured tricks on stupid people; and fortunate indeed was the child or man who won a fairy for his friend.

One day Odin, and his brothers Hoenir and Loki, were walking about on the earth; and as they drew near to the seashore they saw two stately trees, an ash and an elm, standing side by side. Then Odin took the trees, and out of them he made two living beings that resembled the gods themselves in form and feature. Hoenir touched their foreheads, that they might have sight and wisdom, and Loki gave them warm blood, with the power to speak and hear and feel. Thus man and woman were created; and the gods called the man Ask, and the woman Embla, from the names of the trees from which they were made.

2

ODIN'S SEARCH FOR WISDOM

At the end of the rainbow bridge stood the wonderful tree Ygdrasil, which bound all the worlds together in the grasp of its mighty hands. Some of the roots were firmly fixed in Midgard, and even extended underground to the home of the swarthy elves. Some roots branched out into Jötunheim, where the frost-giants ever strove to tear them out; and one root struck down into the very depths of the earth, to that dark region of the dead where ruled the terrible goddess Hel. The Tree of Life also grew upwards to a marvellous height, and its branches spread out so widely that many birds and beasts came to it for shelter. The topmost boughs reached up to Asgard, where they overshadowed Odin's hall.

At the foot of the tree Ygdrasil sat the three Norns – or Fates – who weave the thread of each man's life. Every day the Norns sprinkled the tree with water from the sacred Urdar fountain; so the tree always flourished, and its leaves kept fresh and green in spite of the dragon which forever gnawed at its roots, hoping to

destroy it. The heavy foliage that crowned its upper boughs never lacked for moisture, but grew more beautiful each year, although Heidrun, the goat of Odin, browsed on its leaves, and though it furnished food to four great stags who grazed beside it. From the horns of these stags dew continually fell in such abundance that it supplied water for all the rivers of the earth.

The very topmost branch of the Tree of Life was called the Peace Bough, and on it sat a great eagle who kept watch over all that happened in the worlds below. Up and down the trunk of the mighty Ygdrasil scampered the squirrel Ratatosk, a mischievous little fellow who delighted to make trouble between the eagle and the dragon at the foot of the tree by repeating malicious speeches which he said each had made of the other. In this way he hoped to stir up such strife that he would some day see a terrible battle fought between them. Ratatosk was daring enough to explore all the land that was overshadowed by the boughs of Ygdrasil, but he never ventured near the gates of Asgard, nor did he risk going into the deep grove that sheltered Mimer's well – that wonderful well whose waters flowed down into the roots of the Tree of Life.

The Peace Bough hung over the hall of the gods just above the golden throne where Odin sat ruling the affairs of gods and men. On Odin's head was a shining helmet shaped like an eagle, and over his shoulders was thrown a mantle of deep blue with such a wonderfully jewelled hem that it looked as if the cloak were edged with stars. In his hand he held a spear which was deemed so sacred that if anyone swore an oath upon its point, he would never dare to break it. At Odin's feet crouched two great wolves which he fed daily with his own hand; and on his shoulders perched his two ravens Hugin and Munin (Thought and Memory) who flew each morning over the earth and brought back to Odin the news of all that was going on in the earth below. Sometimes they told him of the brave deeds of heroes; sometimes they spoke of the swarthy elves, or of the frost-giants plotting vengeance in their home beyond the frozen seas; and sometimes they warned him that the Midgard serpent, who lay with his immense body encircling the earth, was lashing the sea into foam with his tail and rolling up the waves until they threatened to cover the earth.

Since the ruling of the world was in Odin's hands, he was anxious to gain wisdom enough for this great task; and though the gods far excelled the earth-folk in knowledge, there were some of the frost-giants who were wiser than Odin, for they knew of things that happened long before the coming of the gods. On this account the dwellers in Asgard were ever fearful lest their enemies should destroy their shining city; and Odin longed for the knowledge that would make him greater than anyone in all the worlds.

There was only one way to get such wisdom as Odin wanted, and that was to drink deep of the water that flowed into Mimer's well. No one save the hoary old giant himself had ever tasted the water of the Well of Wisdom; but Odin knew that without it he could never learn of things past and present and to come. So he laid aside his spear and helmet; and mounting his eight-legged horse Sleipnir, rode over the rainbow bridge to the deep grove of trees in the heart of which old Mimer sat guarding his sacred well.

Leaving Sleipnir some distance behind, Odin advanced alone; and soon came in sight of the giant seated like a stone image beside the Well of Wisdom. Mimer was so very, very old that he looked as if he had sat there ever since the beginning of time; and as Odin stood in the dimly lighted grove, he seemed to be the only living thing in all that vast stillness. The giant's hair was white, and his beard had grown so long that it reached almost to the ground as he leaned forward with his head resting on his hand. In the other hand he held an ivory horn; but though many had passed by the sacred well, no god or mortal had ever been given a drink from Mimer's horn.

Odin advanced slowly to the giant's side; and the old man, who had sat for ages and ages looking down into the clear depths of the water, now raised his eyes and fixed them, not unkindly, on the waiting god. Great and wise as Odin was, being ruler of gods and men, he felt a strange awe in the presence of this hoary old Mimer, who lived long before the creation of the worlds and was living before the gods and the frost-giants engaged in their terrible warfare. As Odin approached the sacred well, Mimer was fully aware of who his visitor was, for he knew all things that ever had been, or are, or were yet to be. His eyes, so keen and piercing, looked kindly upon the god from beneath his shaggy brows; and his voice sounded soft to Odin's ears as he said slowly:–

"What does the All-Father seek so far from sunny Asgard?"

"I have come to beg a draught from your well, O Mimer," answered Odin.

The old giant's face grew grave. "Whoever asks for that," he said, "must be willing to give much in return. Many desire to drink of

the waters of wisdom, but few will pay the price. What will you give in return for a draught from Mimer's well?"

Only a moment did Odin hesitate; then he said boldly, "I will give anything you ask." At these words Mimer handed him the ivory horn, saying: "Drink, then; and the wisdom of the ages shall be yours. But before you go hence, leave with me as a pledge one of your eyes." So Odin drank deep of the well of wisdom; and thereafter no one in all the worlds was able to compare with the Father of the Gods in wisdom. None of the dwellers in Asgard ever questioned Odin concerning his visit to Mimer's well; but they honoured him more deeply for the great sacrifice he had made; and whenever Odin visited the earth to mingle in the affairs of men, people knew him as the god who had but a single eye.

There was one other person besides old Mimer who was reputed to have greater wisdom than the gods, and this was the frost-giant Vafthrudner. Now Odin was very anxious to measure his knowledge with that of his old enemy, for if the frost-giants were no longer wiser than the wisest of the gods, there was less need to fear them. To put his wisdom to the test, Odin set out on the long, dreary journey to Jötunheim; and soon he found Vafthrudner sitting at the door of his snow-house. When the giant saw a visitor approaching, he stopped shaking the icicles from his frozen beard, and stared hard at the intruder. Odin had disguised himself as a traveller, so Vafthrudner did not know him and thought he was another foolish adventurer who had come to learn wisdom at the cost of his life. For the penalty which the loser must pay in his strife with the giant's wisdom was death.

So Vafthrudner laughed until the mountains shook when Odin declared that this was the object of his journey to Jötunheim; for it amused the giant vastly to think that a mere man had come to contend with him in wisdom. He bade the stranger sit down, and Odin obeyed, pulling his slouched hat well over his eye, so that the giant might not guess who his visitor was. "Tell me," said Vafthrudner, "the name of the river that divides Asgard from Jötunheim."

"The river Ifing, where the waters are never frozen," replied Odin, quickly. The frost-giant looked surprised, but he only said:–

"You have answered rightly, O Wise One. And now tell me the names of the horses that draw the chariots of Night and Day."

"Skinfaxe and Hrimfaxe," promptly replied Odin. Vafthrudner turned and looked hard at this remarkable stranger who could speak so readily of things that no man was thought to know. Then he asked many more questions, to which Odin gave unhesitatingly the right answers; and soon the frost-giant began to feel afraid of the strange traveller who seemed to know more than the gods themselves. Anxiously he put the last question, saying, "Tell me, O Great One, the name of the plain on which the Last Battle will be fought." Now Vafthrudner knew that no mortal man could possibly answer this question, so he waited fearfully for Odin's reply.

"On the plain of Vigrid, which is a hundred miles on each side," came the answer; and at this the frost-giant began to quake with fear, for his boasted wisdom had been fairly met, and at last someone had come to Jötunheim to defeat him.

Now it was Odin's turn to ask questions; and he drew from this wisest of the giants a knowledge of things that happened long before the gods came to dwell in Asgard. He learned all the secrets that the giants guarded so carefully; and he made Vafthrudner tell him of the dim unknown future, and of the events that would shape the lives of gods and men. So eager was Odin to gain the desired wisdom that he forgot how long he had been sitting at the frost-giant's side and listening while Vafthrudner told him of the time when no gods were living, and of the time when no gods should be.

The long day waned, and the curious stars peeped out, and Mani – as he drove his horses over the western hills – wondered why Odin lingered so long in dreary Jötunheim. When the All-Father had learned all he desired to know, he rose up and said: "One last question I will put, O Vafthrudner; and by its answer we may judge which is the wiser of us two. What did Odin whisper in the ear of Balder as that shining one lay on the funeral pyre?" When the frost-giant heard this question he knew at last who it was that had been contending with him, and he answered humbly: "Who but thyself, O Odin, can tell the words which thou didst say to thy son? Thou art truly the wisest of all."

So Odin departed on the long journey back to Asgard, and the gods rejoiced at his return, for hitherto no one had ever been known to strive with Vafthrudner and live.

3

THE STORY OF THE MAGIC MEAD

There once lived on the earth a man named Kvasir; and he was much beloved by the gods because they had given him the wonderful gift of poetry. Kvasir was a great traveller, and wherever he went men begged him to tell them, in his singing words, of the life of the gods and of the brave deeds of heroes. So the poet went from cottage to castle sharing his gift with rich and poor alike. Sometimes he told the familiar tales that had grown old on men's lips; and sometimes he sang of heroes in far-off forgotten lands.

Everyone loved Kvasir – everyone except the spiteful little dwarfs who grew jealous of him, and longed to do him some evil. So one day when the poet was walking on the seashore, two of the dwarfs named Fialar and Galar came up to him and begged him to visit their cave in the rocks. Now Kvasir never suspected wrong of anyone, so he willingly followed the dwarfs into a dark cavern underground. Here the treacherous brothers slew him, and drained his blood into three jars in which they had already

placed some honey. Thus of sweetness mingled with a poet's life-blood they brewed the Magic Mead, which would give to anyone who drank of it gentleness and wisdom and the gift of poesy.

When the dwarfs had mixed the mead, they took great care to hide it in a secret cave; and then, proud of their cruel cunning, they set off in search of further adventures. Soon they found the giant Gilling asleep on the seashore; and after pinching him awake, they asked him to row them a little way in his boat. The giant, who was both good-natured and stupid, took the dwarfs into his boat, and began to row vigorously. Then Galar suddenly steered the boat so that it struck on a sharp rock and was overturned. The poor giant, who could not swim, was immediately drowned; while the wicked little dwarfs climbed upon the keel of the boat and finally drifted ashore.

Not content with this cruel act, they went straightaway to the giant's house and called to his wife to come quickly, for Gilling was drowning. The giantess at once hurried to her husband's aid; and as she came through the doorway, Fialar, who had climbed up above the lintel, suddenly dropped a millstone on her head, killing her instantly.

As the dwarfs were jumping up and down exulting over their success, the giant's son – whose name was Suttung – came along. When he saw his mother stretched dead upon the ground, and the little men skipping about in their wicked glee, he guessed who was guilty of this shameful deed. So he seized Galar and Fialar, one in each hand; and, wading far out into the sea, he set them on a certain rock which was sure to be covered with water when the tide rose. As he turned to go away, the dwarfs screamed to him in terror and begged him to take them back to land. In their fright they promised to give him anything he might ask if only he would put them safe on shore.

Now Suttung had heard of the Magic Mead, and he longed very much to possess it; so he made the dwarfs promise to give him the three jars in exchange for their lives. Much as Galar and Fialar hated to do this, they had no choice but to agree to the giant's demand; so as soon as they were on land again, they delivered the precious mead into his hands. As Suttung could not be at home all day to guard his treasure, he hid the jars in a deep recess in the rocks, and bade his daughter Gunlod watch over them night and day. The mouth of the cavern was sealed up with an enormous stone so that no one could enter except by a passageway known only to Gunlod, and Suttung felt that his treasure was safe from both gods and men.

Meanwhile the news of Kvasir's death had been brought to Odin by his ravens Hugin and Munin, and he determined to get possession of the wonderful mead that had been brewed from the poet's blood. So he disguised himself as a traveller, pulled his grey hat well over his face and set out for the country where the Magic Mead was hidden. As he neared the giant's home, he saw a field in which nine sturdy thralls were mowing hay. These men did not belong to Suttung, but were the servants of his brother Baugi. This suited Odin's purpose just as well, so he went quickly up to the thralls and said: "Your scythes seem very dull. How much faster you could work if they were sharper. Shall I whet them for you?" The men were surprised at this

unexpected offer of help; but they accepted the stranger's assistance gladly. When they found how sharp he had made their scythes, they begged him to sell or give them the marvellous whetstone. To this Odin replied, "Whoever can catch it, may have it as a gift," and with these words he threw the stone among them. Then began a fierce battle among the thralls for the possession of the prize; and they cut at each other so fiercely with their scythes that by evening everyone of them lay dead in the field.

While they were fighting thus savagely, Odin sought out Baugi's house and begged for supper and a night's lodging. The giant received him hospitably; and as they sat eating, word was brought to Baugi that his nine thralls were dead. For a time Odin listened to his host's complaints of his evil luck and of how much wealth he would lose through his unmowed fields. Then he offered his services to Baugi, promising to do as much work as the nine thralls. The giant was very doubtful whether his visitor could make good this boast; but he accepted the offer quickly, and next morning Odin set to work in the fields.

Before many days had passed, all the hay on Baugi's land was carefully stored away in the barns, and Odin came to the giant to demand his wages. "What payment shall I make you?" asked Baugi, fearing that a great sum would be named as the price of such remarkable service. He was surprised, therefore, when Odin answered, "All I ask is a draught of the Magic Mead which your brother Suttung keeps hidden in a cavern."

"That is not an easy thing to get," replied the giant, "for though I would be glad to fetch you some of the mead, my brother has never let me enter the cave. However, I will ask him to bring you a single draught." So Baugi went in search of his brother, and told him of the wonderful service that Odin had rendered. Then he asked for one drink of the Magic Mead for his servant. At this Suttung flew into a great rage and cried:

"Do you think I would give any of the mead to a stranger who can do the work of nine thralls? No *man* could have such wonderful power. It is a god that you have been calling your servant, and the gods have been our enemies since the beginning of time."

Now Baugi feared and hated the gods as much as his brother; but he had given his word to Odin to help him get the Magic Mead, and he did not dare to break his promise. So when he returned to his one-time servant, and told of the ill success of his visit to Suttung, Odin answered: "Then we must try some other way. Take me to the cavern where the mead is hidden; but see that your brother knows nothing of our going."

Very unwillingly Baugi consented to show Odin the secret cave; and as they walked, he plotted how to get rid of his troublesome servant. It seemed to take the giant a very long time to find the cavern; but when they finally reached it, Odin drew an augur from his pocket, and began to bore a hole in the great stone that stood at the cave's mouth. As soon as he grew tired, he made Baugi take his turn at the augur; and, owing to the giant's great strength, a hole was soon bored through the rock. Then Odin quickly turned himself into a snake and crept into the opening while Baugi, seeing his servant no longer beside him, and realizing what the sudden transformation meant, made a stab at the snake with the augur,

hoping to kill it. But Odin had slid safely through the hole, and was already inside the cave.

Taking his rightful form, Odin now began to look eagerly about him, and when his eyes grew accustomed to the dimness of the cavern, he saw the daughter of Suttung seated in the furthest corner beside the three jars that contained the Magic Mead. He came softly to Gunlod's side, and spoke to her so gently that she was not frightened at the sudden appearance of a stranger; and when he smiled at her with a reassuring look, she asked, "Who are you, and why are you here?"

"I am a traveller, tired and thirsty after my long journey," answered Odin. "Will you not give me something to drink?"

Gunlod shook her head. "I have nothing here save the Magic Mead, and that I dare not give you," she said sadly. Then Odin begged for just a single draught, but the giant's daughter firmly refused to let him touch the jars.

At last, after much coaxing and soft words, Gunlod allowed her visitor to take one sip of the mead; but as soon as Odin got the jars in his hands, he drained each one dry before the astonished maiden had realized what had happened. Then he changed himself quickly into a snake, and glided out through the opening in the rock. It was now but a moment's work to assume an eagle's form, and start at once on his journey back to Asgard. He knew well that there was no time to lose, for Baugi had already gone to his brother with the news of what had happened at the cave's mouth.

When Suttung heard Baugi's story and realized that his precious mead was being stolen by one of the gods, he hurried at once to the cavern. Just as he reached it, he saw an eagle rise heavily up from the earth, and he knew this was some god in disguise bearing away the Magic Mead to Asgard. So he quickly changed himself into an eagle, and started in pursuit of the one with slowly moving wings. Odin could not fly very fast, for the mead made him heavy; and he was much distressed to see that the giant was easily gaining on him. As they both neared the gates of Asgard, some of the gods were looking out, and they saw the two birds approaching. They wondered what the pursuit might mean; but it was not until the eagles neared the outer walls that the watchers realized that it was Odin fleeing from an enemy, and straining his weary wings to reach Asgard.

Then they laid a great pile of wood on the inner walls, and to this they applied a torch the moment that the first eagle had passed safely over. The flames shot up with a roar just as the pursuer had almost caught his prey. The fire scorched Baugi's great wings, and the smoke blinded his eyes so that he fluttered helplessly down to the earth. Meanwhile the Magic Mead was safe in Asgard, and there it was put in care of Bragi, the white-haired son of Odin. Thus the mead remained forever with the gods; but sometimes a favoured mortal is given, at his birth, a drop of this divine drink; and then, in later years, men find that a poet has been born among them.

4

GODS AND MEN

I

Near Odin's council hall was a fair white building called the Hall of Mists, and here sat Frigga, the wife of Odin, spinning the many-coloured clouds. She spent long hours beside her golden wheel; and when she spun by day, the clouds were white and soft and fleecy; but toward evening Frigga put a touch of colour into her work, and then the heavens glowed with yellow and violet and red. It was through Odin's careful wife that snow fell plentifully in winter, for then Frigga shook her feather beds, and made them ready for the touch of the spring sunshine. At her command the rain fell all through the year, so that the streets of Asgard might always be kept spotless. It was Frigga, too, who made the wonderful gift of flax to men; and she taught the women how to spin and weave.

Frigga was very fond of children; and one day, as she looked down upon the earth, she saw two little boys playing together on the seashore. They were Geirrod and Agnar, sons of a wealthy king; and Frigga grew to love them very dearly. She was so anxious to talk to them and know them, that she persuaded Odin to go with her down to the earth; and, having disguised themselves as an old fisherman and his wife, they took possession of a deserted hut. This hut was on an island many miles from the country where Geirrod and Agnar lived; but Odin promised Frigga that in spite of this, the children would come to her.

One day Geirrod and his brother went out rowing in their boat, and a storm came up which blew the tiny craft far out to sea. The boys became terribly frightened; and the wind tossed them about on the angry waves until they would surely have perished if Odin had not been watching over them. He kept their frail boat from sinking, and guided it to the very shore on which he and Frigga were living in the little hut. The boys were glad indeed when their feet once more touched the solid earth; for they were tired and hungry and cold, and a good deal frightened, too. They knew that they must be far from their own country; but they were so glad to be out of reach of the waves that it mattered little to them what land it was to which the wind had brought them.

When they began to look about them, they found that the island was very bleak and bare, with no flowers nor fruits nor berries to be seen anywhere. Nothing seemed to be growing there but low, thorny bushes that scratched them and tore their clothes as they attempted to make their way further into the island. Soon

it began to get dark, and the boys stumbled helplessly through the briers; but at last they saw the glimmer of a light, and groped their way toward it. Presently they came to a small hut, through whose open window the friendly light was streaming, and, without a moment's hesitation, they knocked loudly at the door.

They were a bit surprised at the appearance of the two people within the hut; for although they were simply clad as peasants, there was something in their bearing that reminded Geirrod and Agnar of the lordly guests who had sat at their father's table. But the boys were too hungry and tired to pay much attention to the kind folk who took them in, though they were grateful for the food and dry clothing and a warm place by the fire. Some days later, Geirrod inquired of his host how a fisherman could afford such wonderfully soft beds and food fit for kings to dine upon. Agnar asked no questions, but wondered why the flowers bloomed so plentifully around the cottage door, and why the birds sang all day.

It was too stormy for the boys to attempt to venture on the sea for many days; and even when the storm was over, the waves looked dark and menacing. Winter was coming on, and there was little chance that the sea would grow calm; so Geirrod and Agnar lingered day after day in the fisherman's cottage, needing no persuasion to remain with their new-found friends. Geirrod spent all of his time with the fisherman, learning the lore of the sea and becoming very adept in the use of the spear as well as the humbler net and line. He was also taught to hunt the game that was plentiful on the island, and he grew very proud of his skill with the bow. All day he stayed at the fisherman's side,

listening, learning and wondering at the great knowledge which his companion had of things that had happened before the world was made. He heard many tales of heroes, and learned of brave deeds that had been done by men of his own race. He knew that the fisherman told these stories so that he himself might see how fine a thing it was to be brave and strong and noble; and Geirrod, who was by nature selfish and cruel, felt so thrilled by the old man's stirring words that he wished to be like the heroes whose lives were so loudly praised.

Agnar usually stayed with the fisherman's wife in the cottage; for he was gentler and more timid than his brother, and preferred to help his kind foster-mother instead of hunting with Geirrod or venturing out on the sea to spear the great fish. Agnar, too, heard many stories as he sat by the goodwife's side while she spun her flax; but these were not hero-tales nor stories of adventure. She told him how the god Freyr makes the flowers bloom, and the fruits ripen; and how his sister Freya watches over the earth all through the springtime. She spoke of the love which these two had for all the beautiful things in nature, for music and poetry, and how they even watched with delight the dancing of the fairies in Elfheim. She told him how wonderful the city of Asgard looked when the sun shone on the broad, golden streets; and how the sounds re-choed through the great hall called Valhalla where Odin feasted with the heroes chosen from the battlefield.

So the winter passed quickly, and when spring came the fisherman built a new, strong boat in which the boys were to make their voyage homeward. Then Geirrod and Agnar said

goodbye to the kind folk with whom they had passed so many happy days. Reluctantly they sailed away from the friendly island, and soon came in sight of their own country. A fair wind carried them gently all the way, for Odin had commanded Njord, the storm god, to keep his blusterous winds under control. As the boat neared the familiar shores, Geirrod forgot all the generous lessons that the fisherman had tried to teach him, and he began to look with hatred at his brother. As Agnar was the older of the two, he would inherit the kingdom; so Geirrod was filled with a sudden rage against the gentle boy who stood in the way of his becoming king.

As the boat drew toward the shore, Geirrod sprang out, and giving the boat a mighty shove toward the open sea he cried: "Go back to the island, you weak, timid creature. You are not fit to be king." Then, being a sturdy swimmer, he made for the land. The boat drifted out again to sea, and carried Agnar to a strange land, where he lived many years. Finally he returned to his own country in disguise and became a servant in his father's palace – but by this time Geirrod had already been made king. For when Geirrod swam ashore, he hastened at once to his father and told him the whole story of his adventure with the fisherman on the island. When the king asked for Agnar, Geirrod said that his brother had been drowned on the journey home by falling over the edge of the boat. As there was no reason to doubt this story, the king mourned for Agnar as one dead; and the younger brother was acknowledged heir to the throne. Not many years later, the king died and Geirrod was made ruler over the whole kingdom.

When Odin and Frigga, who had long since left the island and returned to Asgard, learned what had become of their favourites, Odin was very proud that Geirrod had become a great king. Frigga grieved, however, that the gentle Agnar had suffered through his brother's treachery, and hated to see him serving as a menial in Geirrod's hall. When Odin praised his former pupil, she would say: "He is a great king, but a cruel man. No stranger would dare to trust to his mercy."

Now as unkindness to a stranger was a very despicable trait in those days, this taunt of Frigga's roused Odin's wrath; and he determined to show her that Geirrod was not the heartless king she declared him to be. So he disguised himself as an aged traveller, and presented himself at Geirrod's palace asking for food and shelter. Frigga, however, was equally determined to prove Geirrod's cruelty, and thus defend her favourite, Agnar. So she secretly sent a messenger to the king bidding him beware of a strange old man who would come to the palace claiming the rights of hospitality.

Odin was much surprised when he met with rough usage at the hands of Geirrod's servants, not knowing that the king had commanded them to seize any aged traveller who might come to the palace. He was not welcomed to the well-filled table as he had expected, but was rudely dragged before the king. Now Geirrod, believing that this was the stranger of whom he had been warned to beware, commanded the old man to tell his name and the object of his visit. The traveller stood with bowed head, refusing to speak; and this made the king so angry that he threatened the old man with torture and death if he did not answer.

As the stranger continued to keep silent, Geirrod commanded his servants to chain him to a pillar in the great hall and build on each side of him a hot fire whose flames would torture without destroying him. So they dragged the unresisting old man to the pillar and bound him with chains too strong for even the stoutest warrior to break. Then they kindled fires on either side of him and stood off, laughing and mocking at the trembling figure that seemed to crouch in terror against the pillar.

For eight days and nights the fires were kept burning, and during all this time the cruel king allowed no meat or drink to be given to his prisoner. But one night, when the watchers were drowsy with ale and the heat of the fires, a servant stole softly into the hall with a great drinking-horn in his hand. This he carried to the old man, who appeared to be in great suffering, and he smiled happily when he saw the prisoner drain the cool drink to the last drop. This servant was Agnar, the king's brother, whom everyone believed to be dead.

The next morning, Geirrod assembled all his nobles in the great hall, and they began to make merry over the prisoner's misery, asking him if he would now speak and tell them who he was and from whence he came. The old man shook his head, refusing to speak; but suddenly, to the astonishment of all, he began to sing. And as he sang, the listeners grew strangely silent, while a nameless fear seized the whole company as they saw no longer the crouching figure by the pillar, but a tall commanding form before whose awful majesty they shrank back trembling and afraid. As the singing continued, the power and sweetness of the music

filled the echoing halls; and when the song was over, the chains fell suddenly from the prisoner's arms and he stood – a terrible accusing power – before the eyes of the terrified people. Geirrod as well as his nobles knew now that a god had come among them; and the king, fearing for his life, tried madly to defend himself. He seized his sword and rushed blindly at the tall form confronting him, forgetting – in his terror – that no weapon could prevail against an immortal. Blinded by his fury, he fell forward upon his own sword, and in a moment lay dead at Odin's feet.

Then the All-Father called to Agnar and bade him take his rightful place on the throne which his brother had usurped. The people gladly welcomed a kindlier ruler; and Odin, having righted the wrongs which Geirrod's cruelty had created, now returned to Asgard to report to the anxious Frigga that her favourite was at last made king.

II

There was once a king named Gylfe who was reputed to be the wisest ruler of his time. He kept many learned men at his court; but he was eager to gain more knowledge than all these sages could command, and so sent far and wide for men skilled in magic and those whose eyes could read the secrets of the stars.

One day an old woman came to Gylfe's palace asking alms, and she was brought at once into the presence of the king. Gylfe treated her with great kindness, and while she sat at the king's table

eating of his own rich food, she turned to the monarch saying: "Never has the stranger met with such kindness as this. What can I give you in return?" The guests who were feasting began to laugh merrily, but the king answered, "There is nothing that I wish for except wisdom." "Then, listen," said the strange old woman, and she began to tell the king a story of the world as it was when it came fresh from the hands of the gods. Then she spoke of the frost-giants, the ancient enemies of the shining ones of Asgard; and as the king listened, he seemed to see how all things must have looked in that first morning of the world.

When the old woman finished speaking and turned to leave the palace, Gylfe begged her to accept some gift in return for her wonderful stories; and the stranger, who was really a giantess, replied: "I will take as much land as four oxen can plough in a day and a night." Now the frost-giants had been envying the earth-folk many years, and they wished to add more land to their country beyond the frozen seas. So when Gylfe consented to the old woman's strange request, she brought four immense oxen from Jötunheim, and harnessed them to a huge plough. Then the giantess cut such a deep furrow into the earth that a great tract of land was torn away; and this, being carried out to sea by the oxen, was borne westward to Jötunheim. Thus Gylfe lost a large part of his kingdom, but he felt that even that was not too great a price to pay for the knowledge which he had gained.

Having learned from the giantess how wise were all the dwellers in Asgard, Gylfe determined to seek the gods themselves; though he knew that in his eager desire for more wisdom he was likely to

41

meet death at their hands for his presumption. So he set out on the journey to Asgard; but he would surely have never reached those sacred halls if Odin had not guided his footsteps and led him to the rainbow bridge that reached up from Midgard to the city of the gods. Here, at the end of Bifrost, he met Heimdall, the watchman who stood all day and night guarding the shining city from the approach of the giants. Whenever a stranger appeared at the rainbow bridge he sounded his horn to warn the gods of possible danger. Heimdall never slept; and he not only saw as well by night as by day, but his eyes had the wonderful power of seeing a hundred miles all around. He also had such remarkable ears that he could hear the grass growing, and tell whether the wind was blowing on the sea.

Having received a command from Odin to let the stranger pass, Heimdall allowed the king to enter the sacred city; and Gylfe soon found himself in the presence of Odin. The Father of the Gods received him kindly; and, after learning the object of his journey, permitted Gylfe to seat himself in the great council-hall. Then Odin asked the king what it was he wished to know, and Gylfe began to question him freely and fearlessly. He asked about the creation of the world, about the seasons and the rainfalls, and the changes of the moon. He asked why the elves kept themselves forever hidden in the earth, and why the fairies danced only in the moonlight. He spoke, though timidly, of the dark underworld, and asked why the dead never came back to earth again. He even questioned Odin concerning the gods themselves; and to all these eager queries, the All-Father gave a willing answer.

Suddenly the hall grew full of mist and shadows, and Gylfe could hardly see the foot of Odin's throne. A great noise like some deafening thunder shook the council-hall, and the king, bewildered and frightened, did not know where to turn for safety. Then all at once the darkness and the sounds vanished, and Gylfe found himself on a broad plain. At first he thought that he had seen the shield-hung hall and the shining streets of Asgard only in a dream; but soon the words of Odin came back to him, and he knew that he had indeed talked with the greatest of the gods.

So Gylfe became the wisest ruler on the earth; but though all men honoured him for his great wisdom, many refused to believe that he had really been within the gates of Asgard.

5

SIF'S GOLDEN HAIR AND THE MAKING OF THE HAMMER

I

Among the gods there was one who was really unfit to be a god and to live in the shining city of Asgard. He was the cause of much trouble and mischief in his frequent journeys to the earth, and he brought evil upon even the gods themselves. But as Loki was the brother of Odin, he could not very well be banished from Asgard, so the gods endured his presence as best they could. Loki did many unkind things that the gods never heard of; but once he met with just punishment for his meanness. This was the time that he robbed Sif of her golden hair.

Sif was the wife of Thor, the god of thunder. She had beautiful long hair that fell over her shoulders like a shower of gold, and

of this she was very proud. One day Sif fell asleep on the steps of Thor's palace, and while she lay there sleeping Loki came walking by. There was nothing so dear to Loki as a chance to do mischief, and he never saw anything beautiful without wishing to spoil it; so when he found Sif fast asleep, he stole up softly behind her and cut off all her golden hair.

When Sif woke at last and saw what had happened, she began to cry bitterly, for her golden hair was the pride and joy of Thor, and she was afraid that he would never want to look at her again now that it was gone. So she got up from the steps where she was sitting, and went away to hide in the garden. When Thor came home, he looked for her all through the palace, and went from room to room calling her name. Not finding her in the house, he went out into the garden, and after searching for a long time finally found poor Sif behind a stone, sobbing bitterly. When he heard her story, he tried to comfort her the best he could, but Sif continued weeping and covered her shorn head with her arms.

"I know who did this shameful thing," cried Thor, wrathfully; "it was that mischief-maker Loki, but this time he shall pay dearly for his wickedness." And he strode out of the palace with a look so threatening that even the gods might have trembled before him. Now Loki was not expecting to be caught so soon, and he had not thought of seeking a hiding place; so when Thor came suddenly upon him he was too frightened to try to escape. He even forgot his ready lies, and when Thor shook him angrily and threatened to kill him for his wicked act, he made no denial, only begged for mercy and promised to restore to Sif the hair he had cut off.

Thor therefore released him, after binding him by a solemn oath to fulfil his promise.

The real hair which Loki had cut off he had already lost, so to keep his word to Thor he must find something else which would resemble it closely enough to make Sif believe she had indeed her own hair again. As there was only one place where skilful and cunning work like this could be done, Loki crossed the rainbow bridge that spans the gulf between Asgard and the earth, and hurried to the tall mountain which hides, amid its rocks, the entrance to the lower world. No one but a god, or one of the swarthy elves themselves, could have found this hidden opening, but Loki knew it well. He first looked for a tiny stream which flowed along at the foot of the mountain. This he followed to its source in a deep cave among the rocks, and when he came to the spot where it bubbled up from the ground, he raised a huge log that was lying, apparently by chance, close beside it. This disclosed a small passage leading down into the very centre of the earth, and along this path Loki hastened, often stumbling about in the darkness, until he came to the underworld where lived the swarthy elves. They were busily engaged in their wonderful workshop, which was lighted only by the fires from the forge, but when they saw Loki they laid down their tools and asked him how they could serve him.

"I have a task," answered Loki, "which requires such great skill to perform that I hardly dare ask you to attempt it. It is nothing less than for you to make of your gold some locks of hair that will be as soft and fine and beautiful as the golden hair which adorns

the head of Sif, the wife of Thor. You have heard, no doubt, of its beauty, so you know how difficult a task I have given you."

The elves, nothing daunted, set at once to work, and selecting a bar of perfect gold, they pounded it very soft, then spun it into threads so fine that they looked like sunbeams, and so soft that they felt like silk. When the work was finished and placed in Loki's hand, it exceeded in beauty anything he had ever seen, and he felt sure that Thor could not complain of his gift. Then he thanked the swarthy elves and hastened with his prize back to Asgard and to the palace of Thor, where all the gods had assembled to see the fulfilment of Loki's promise.

In spite of the success of his undertaking, the fear of Thor's hasty temper kept Loki somewhat humbled, for the Thunderer had been known to crush the object of his anger with his hammer when once his wrath was fully roused. His face was now dark and threatening as Loki approached, and beside him stood Sif, weeping bitterly, and trying to cover her head with her hands. But Loki came up boldly and placed the golden hair which the elves had made, upon her head. To the astonishment of all, it immediately grew fast, and no one could have told that it was not her own golden hair. So Sif was proud and happy once again, and Loki was forgiven.

II

When Loki went to the underground home of the elves to find the golden hair for Sif, he thought that it would be as well to get two other gifts – one for Odin and one for Freyr – so that their anger would fall less heavily on him for his cruelty to Thor's beautiful wife. The dwarfs were always very glad to help Loki when he was in trouble, for they, too, delighted in mischief-making; so when he asked them for the two other gifts, they gladly set to work. The spun-gold hair they had already placed in Loki's hands; and now they hurried about, getting together a hundred different materials to use in their work – for things of earth, air, fire and water went into the making of the wonderful gifts that came from the hands of the elves.

In a short time they handed to the waiting god a spear that would always hit the mark no matter how badly it was thrown, and a marvellous boat that would fold up into a tiny package, but could also expand large enough to hold all the gods and goddesses in Asgard. Loki was delighted with these gifts and hurried with them back to Odin's council-hall where the gods had assembled to pass judgment on him for his cruel treatment of Sif.

Though the hair of spun gold proved to be so perfect that Loki had nothing to fear from Thor's anger, he saw that Odin was still displeased and was looking at him with stern brows. So the wily god produced his two other gifts, and handed the spear to Odin and the boat to Freyr. Both the gods were delighted with the clever workmanship of the elves; and all the company were so busy examining Loki's gifts that they did not notice the dwarf Brock, who had followed Loki to Asgard and was now standing in the shadow of Odin's throne.

When the gods grew loud in their approval of the magic spear and boat, Brock could contain his anger no longer and cried out:

"Can you find nothing better than those petty toys to praise? My brother Sindri can make far more wonderful things than these." At this boastful interference Loki grew very angry and said: "Prove it, then; for I know that your brother is only a stupid workman. Let us make a wager that you cannot bring here three gifts better than those you scorn; and whichever of us loses in the contest shall pay for it with his head." Brock accepted the challenge and set off at once to the cave where Sindri kept his dwarfs at work night and day.

He told his brother of the wager he had made with Loki, and Sindri laughed and promised that the god's head should hang that night in the cave as a trophy. Then he made ready a huge fire, and as he worked busily over his tools he bade Brock keep the bellows going as hard as he could so that the flames would leap higher and higher. Then, when he thought the right moment had come, he threw into the fire a pigskin; and bidding Brock keep steadily at work on the bellows, he left the cave.

The dwarf blew hard at the fire, and the forge gleamed so brightly that the whole cave was lit up, and Brock could see the piles of gold and silver and glittering gems that lay all around. Then suddenly an enormous gadfly flew into the room; and, lighting on his hand, stung him so badly that he roared with pain. Still he did not take his hand from the bellows, for, with the cunning of his race, he knew that the gadfly was none other than Loki who had taken this form, hoping to spoil Sindri's work.

When the master-smith returned, he looked eagerly at the forge and saw that the fire glowed as brightly as ever. So he muttered a few magic words over the flames and drew forth a golden boar. This he handed to his brother, saying that the boar had the power to fly through the air, and shed light from his golden bristles as he flew. Brock was so much pleased with this gift that he said nothing about his swollen hand; and when Sindri asked him to keep his place at the bellows, he willingly agreed.

The smith then threw a lump of gold into the flames; and bidding Brock keep the fire at white heat, he again left the cave. Brock began to work harder than ever at the bellows; and as the fire glowed so that it seemed like daylight in the room, the gadfly flew at him and stung him on the neck. He screamed with pain and tried to shake off his tormentor, but still he kept faithfully at his work and never lifted his hand a moment from the bellows. When Sindri returned, he found the fire glowing brightly, and, leaning over it, he pulled out of the flames a fine gold ring, which every ninth night would drop nine gold rings as wonderful as itself.

Brock was so delighted with this gift that he almost forgot about his wounded neck; and obediently kept his place at the bellows. Then Sindri threw a lump of iron into the fire, and bidding his brother work steadily at his task – for this was the most important gift of all – he went out of the cave. Brock grasped the bellows firmly, and began to work with all his might. Just as the flames were leaping fiercely and the room seemed lit by a million candles, the gadfly flew at Brock and stung him between the eyes.

The poor little dwarf was almost frantic from the pain of the wound and from the blood that poured into his eyes. But though dazed and blinded so that he could hardly see the fire,

he kept doggedly at work on the bellows, only lifting one hand for a moment to wipe the blood from his eyes. The fire had been glowing like a furnace, but in that one instant the flames burned less brightly, and Sindri – who had just entered the room – began to berate his brother for his carelessness. Then the smith drew out of the fire a mighty hammer, perfect in every way except that the handle was too short, owing to Brock's having lifted his hand a moment from the bellows.

Sindri gave the three gifts to his brother, and bade him hasten to Asgard, and bring back the head of Loki as payment for the lost wager. When the dwarf reached Odin's council-hall, the gods had assembled to decide the contest, for everyone was eager to see what gifts Sindri had sent. Brock handed the ring to Odin, who praised it highly and said, "Now, I shall never want for gold." Freyr was delighted with his gift of the golden boar and said that it would be much more entertaining to ride on its back than in Loki's magic boat. Lastly Brock gave the wonderful hammer Mjölner to Thor, saying, "Here is a hammer which can crush mountains, can cause lightning and thunder when it swings through the air, and will always come back to your hand no matter how far you may throw it." Then the dwarf turned to Odin and said, "Decide now between Loki and me, O Wise One, and declare whose gifts are worth most to Asgard."

Though the gods were reluctant to condemn one of their number in favour of a dwarf, there was no disputing the fact that Thor's hammer was worth more than all of Loki's gifts, for it meant a sure protection to Asgard from the attacks of the frost-giants.

So Odin declared that Brock had won the wager, and that Loki must pay the forfeit with his head. Now Loki had no intention of submitting to this decree, so he first offered the dwarf a huge sum of money as a ransom; but Brock angrily refused the gold, and insisted that the bargain should be kept. Then Loki cried out, "Well, you must catch me first," and sped off on his magic shoes, which could carry him through the air and over the water with wonderful swiftness. As Brock knew he could never catch the fugitive, he grew black with rage, and turned upon Odin, crying, "Is this the way that the gods keep faith, or shall the word of Odin stand fast?" Now all the company knew well that a promise made by even the meanest among them must be held sacred; so Odin sent Thor after Loki. In his swift chariot, drawn by the snow-white goats, the Thunderer easily overtook the runaway and brought him back to Asgard. Then Loki saw that he must save his life by cunning, and he said to Brock, "You may take my head if you wish, but you must not touch my neck."

Now as this was obviously impossible, the dwarf knew that he was outwitted by the crafty Loki, so he went away fuming with rage and disappointment. But before he left Asgard, he took out of his pocket an awl and a thong, and sewed Loki's lips together so that, for a while at least, the tricky god could not do any more boasting.

6

THE BINDING OF THE FENRIS WOLF

In the very beginning of time, when the gods first made the world, there was joy and gladness not only in Asgard but over all the earth; sin and evil were unknown, and death had not yet come even among men. So the gods were very happy – all except Loki, who looked on with jealous eyes at the gladness which he could not share; for he knew no pleasure except in devising mischief. Not satisfied with grudging others their happiness, he sought some means to bring about trouble, but finding himself too powerless to accomplish anything alone, he married a fierce giantess and had three terrible children – Hel, the Midgard serpent and Fenrer, the Fenris wolf.

These dreadful creatures soon grew very strong and fearful to look upon; and Loki was not content to keep them in the dark cave in Jötunheim with their gruesome mother, but allowed them to roam about the earth. Soon they wearied of the narrow limits of the earth and found no longer any pleasure in bringing terror and

even death to many lands. So Loki took them up to Asgard and begged the gods to let him keep them there. For a while all went well, but soon the presence of Loki's children became a menace to even the gods' safety; and they grew fearful of Hel's deadly eyes, and the serpent's foaming mouth and Fenrer's cruel jaws.

So one day Odin rose up from his throne, stern and wrathful, and cast Hel down into the centre of the earth, to rule over the dark region of the dead. Then he threw the Midgard serpent into the bottom of the sea, where he grew larger and larger, until his huge body encircled the whole earth. But before he could banish Fenrer, Loki came forward and begged that the wolf might be spared and allowed to remain, promising the gods that he would see that it did no harm. So Odin consented, though with doubt and mistrust.

After a while the wolf became very large and fierce, and nothing seemed to appease his savage hunger. Only Tyr, the sword-god, dared feed him, and he wandered about Asgard growing daily more hungry, and more cruel and terrible to see. At length Odin called the gods together in council and said to them:–

"Fenrer is getting to be more of a menace to our lives every day, and I no longer trust Loki's promise to guard our safety. We must therefore find some way to control the wolf, for we cannot kill him and so stain our shining city with his blood."

Then Thor proposed that they should bind Fenrer with a strong chain which he himself would make; and to this plan the gods gladly agreed. So all that night and for many days to come the sound of Thor's hammer could be heard throughout Asgard as he forged the links of a massive chain that should bind the Fenris wolf. When it was finished, the gods assembled before Odin, Thor carrying the heavy chain upon his shoulders, and Loki coming up cautiously with Fenrer, who stalked boldly beside him. No force could possibly be used with a creature so strong and fierce, so the gods sought to gain their end by flattery, praising the wolf's size and strength, and daring him to match it against the strength of the chain which Thor had made.

Now Fenrer knew far better than they how terribly strong he had become, and therefore he willingly lay down and let them fasten the chain around his great body, and then secure it to a rock. When this was done, the gods breathed more freely, for it seemed as if they had nothing to fear from the wolf any longer; but in a moment Fenrer rose, stretched his huge limbs and shook himself once. As he did so, the chain fell to pieces as easily as if it were made of glass. The gods looked on in wonder and dismay, and the wolf walked off with a low, threatening growl. Even Odin was silent with fear, for it had been revealed to him in the runes that in the final overthrow of Asgard, the Fenris wolf should bear a part.

Thor now came forward and begged permission to try again at making another chain much larger and stronger than the last. The forging of this second chain took many days and nights, for Thor tested every link to see that it was strong and sure. At last it was finished, and brought on the shoulders of the strongest of the gods to the foot of Odin's throne. Fenrer was again summoned, but when he saw the chain, he refused to be bound. No flattery or coaxing could move him, so the gods began to taunt him, laughing at his

boasted strength and accusing him of cowardice. Apparently with great reluctance, the wolf again allowed himself to be bound; and when the chain was secured about his shaggy body and fastened tightly to the ground, the gods looked on, feeling fearful and yet full of joy, for surely nothing could be stronger than the massive chain which was wound round and round the prostrate wolf. But Fenrer rose slowly, stretched himself, and gave one bound into the air, while the gods drew back in dismay before the rattling shower of broken links.

Then Odin saw that no brass or steel or any metal could withstand the terrible strength of the wolf, and he bade Thor give up all further attempts to forge a chain, while he had it proclaimed throughout Asgard that Fenrer was to roam wherever he would. Shortly after this he sent Loki on a journey far across the seas to a country so distant from Asgard that he would have to be gone many days. Though usually alert and suspicious, Loki set off on his errand, not dreaming that Odin had some purpose in sending him away. As soon as he was gone, Odin despatched Skirner, Freyr's trusty servant, with all speed to the home of the swarthy elves, and bade him procure from them an enchanted chain, such as they alone knew how to make. Skirner set out at once and found his journey a safer and pleasanter one than he had expected, for though the home of the elves was underground, the road was easy to find. Odin had instructed him to look at the base of a certain mountain for a tiny stream of opal-tinted water. Having come to the foot of the mountain, Skirner followed the stream to its rocky source, and the rest of the journey was quickly made.

When he delivered his message to the elves, they set immediately to work, and for nine days and nights Skirner heard no sound in the workshop as the little men plied their task. No stroke of hammer or noise of anvil was necessary in the making of this wonderful chain, for into its weaving went the strangest things that Skirner had ever seen – the down from a butterfly's wing, a handful of moonbeams, the lace of a spider's web, a humming bird's lance, the breath of the night wind and many other queer and mysterious things. The work was all done in perfect silence, and Skirner sat by looking on in wonder as the magic chain grew into being under the elves' skilful fingers. At last it was finished, and with the precious gift in his hands, Skirner hastened back to Asgard.

Then Odin called the gods together and summoned Fenrer to come and try his strength a third time. When the wolf saw the chain which was to bind him, he became at once suspicious, especially when he found that Loki was absent. He had no doubt of his power to break brass and steel, but he scented a possible danger in the soft, fine thread which lay in Odin's hand. As he had no one here to warn him if the gods meant mischief, he felt that it was safer to wait until Loki was present; so he drew away, growling and showing his teeth. At this Thor cried out –

"How now, Fenrer, have you used up all your strength in breaking those heavy chains, and have not enough left to snap this slender thread?"

This taunt made the wolf growl more fiercely than ever, though he consented a third time to be bound, demanding first,

however, that one of the gods should put his hand in the wolf's huge mouth, and leave it there as a pledge that no magic arts were being used against him. None of the gods wished to take such a risk, and they all drew back in dismay except Tyr, the sword-god, who stepped boldly forward and thrust his hand into the wolf's mouth. Then Fenrer submitted to be bound, and allowed the gods to wind the slender thread all about him and fasten the end to a rock. The moment it was secured, the wolf tried as before to shake himself free, but the more he struggled and strained, the tighter grew the magic thread, until at last Fenrer lay bound and helpless and foaming madly with rage. Seeing that he had been tricked, he closed his teeth savagely upon Tyr's fingers, and bit off his whole hand. But the sword-god felt repaid for the loss of his hand since the wolf at last was bound. Thus the gods left him securely chained to the rock; and there he lay until the final terrible day when it was decreed that he should break loose again, and help in bringing destruction upon all the dwellers of Asgard.

7

HOW THOR WENT FISHING

One day the gods went to a feast given by Aeger the sea-god; and they drank so much ale that before the meal was half over the vessel which old Aeger had filled was drained dry. He was greatly distressed at finding there was not enough to drink, and he began at once to brew more of the foaming ale. As his kettle was rather small for so great a company, he asked Thor to find him a larger one that would better suit the needs of the gods. To this Thor, who was always ready for any sort of adventure, replied readily –

"Tell me where to get the kettle, and I will fetch it, even if it is from the very heart of Jötunheim."

Now Aeger had no idea where to look for such an enormous kettle as he needed; but just then Tyr spoke up and said:–

"My father Hymer has a kettle that is one mile deep and half a mile wide. If Thor wishes to risk the giant's anger, he can go with me to Hymer's castle."

So the two gods set off for their long journey in Thor's swift goat-chariot; and though they travelled quickly over the frost-bound country that stretched far away to the north, it was a long time before they came to the land where Hymer and his kindred lived. Here they had to cross two half-frozen rivers over which the goats carried them safely, and then they came to the foot of a great ice-covered mountain that looked as smooth as glass. Tyr advised that they go the rest of the way on foot; so, leaving the chariot by some low fir trees, the two gods proceeded to climb up the slippery side of the mountain.

Almost at the top they came upon Hymer's castle, and they entered the spacious hall where a huge fire, made of entire trees, was burning on the hearth. Near the fire was seated Tyr's grandmother, a hideous old giantess who did not speak to the two gods as they entered, but only grinned horridly at them, showing her long, pointed teeth that looked like a wolf's fangs. Beside her sat a beautiful woman spinning flax with a golden wheel. This was Tyr's mother, who was as lovely as the old woman was hideous, and as kind as the hag was cruel. She welcomed her son affectionately, but warned him that both he and Thor had better keep hidden until they found out whether Hymer was disposed to be friendly – for when the giant was angry he was not a pleasant person to encounter.

Late in the evening Hymer came home, tired and ill-tempered after an unsuccessful day's fishing. He shook the snow from his clothes and combed the ice out of his long, white beard. Then he sat down by the fire, and while he watched the meat turn on the spit, Tyr's mother said softly: "Our son has come to see you. Shall we welcome him to the fire?" Before Hymer could answer, the old giantess croaked out, "And Thor has come with him – the strongest god in Asgard and the enemy of our race."

Hymer looked very angry as he heard this, and when his old mother cried, "Look, they are hiding behind the furthest pillar," the giant stared at the pillar with such a piercing look that it cracked in two. Then the beam overhead suddenly snapped, and the kettles that were hanging from it fell with a crash to the floor. There were eight of these kettles, and among them was the huge one of which Tyr had spoken to the sea-god. All of the kettles were broken by the fall except the largest; and as Hymer was stooping to pick this up, Tyr and Thor walked out from behind the pillar.

The giant was not very well pleased to see Thor, but as the visitor came in company with his son, he decided to treat him civilly. So he invited the two gods to come and eat with him, and made a place for them by the fire. There were three oxen served for supper; and after Thor had eaten two of them and started on a third, Hymer cried:–

"Ho, there! If you eat all our meat, you will have to catch us some fish tomorrow." Thor laughed and replied that he was only too glad of a chance to go fishing. So next morning when the giant set off at sunrise, Thor went with him to the beach, and watched him get the lines and the nets ready. "If I am to catch the fish, will you give me some bait?" he asked, and Hymer replied with a growl, "Go and find some for yourself."

So Thor went over to the meadow where the giant's cattle were grazing, and, seizing the largest bull by the neck, he wrung off its head, and carried this down to the boat. Hymer was very angry at this treatment of his property, but he said nothing, only bade Thor take the oars. Then he gave the boat a great shove, and sprang in with such violence that the whole craft was almost overturned.

Under Thor's quick strokes the boat shot over the water like an arrow, and the giant looked a bit surprised to see how well his companion could pull. With every dip of the oars the boat gathered speed, and they very soon reached Hymer's fishing ground. He then called to Thor to stop rowing, but the god only shook his head and pulled all the harder. In a few moments they were out of sight of land, and the boat was swinging heavily in the trough of the sea. Hymer begged Thor not to go any farther, but the god laughed and said –

"There is much better fishing a few miles ahead." Then he bent hard at the oars, and the boat flew over the waves with incredible swiftness. Soon Hymer began to be frightened, and called loudly, "If you go much farther, we shall be over the Midgard serpent."

Now this was just what Thor intended; so he kept on rowing until they were just over the spot where the huge snake lay coiled at the bottom of the ocean with his tail in his mouth. Then Thor drew in his oars and began to bait his line with the bull's head. Hymer had his things all ready for fishing, and as soon as he dropped his line into the sea the bait was grabbed with a sudden jerk which nearly toppled the giant overboard. Regaining his balance, he proudly pulled up out of the water two whales, and flung them in the boat. Then Thor threw out his line, and in a moment the whole sea was in an uproar, for the bait had been seized by the Midgard serpent and the hook was now caught fast in its great mouth.

When Thor felt the terrible pull on his line, he grasped it with all his might, and braced himself against the side of the boat. The serpent was indeed a match for him in strength, and Thor – to prevent being dragged out into the water – set himself with such force against the framework of the boat that his feet broke right through, and he found himself standing on the bottom of the sea. Here he could take such firm hold that he was able to draw the serpent up to the edge of the boat. The monster lashed the waves fiercely with its tail, and churned the water into foam as it writhed about in its efforts to get free from the torturing hook. Its great head rose above the boat's side, and in its struggles the beast looked more terrifying than when its glittering eyes and great coiled body frightened the dwellers in Asgard.

But Thor was determined not to let the serpent go, so he only pulled the harder and the sea became a great whirlpool of blood and foam and tossing waves. Hymer, who had been looking on in amazement at Thor's strength, now sprang forward and cut the line just as the god was raising his hammer to crush the monster's head. The Midgard serpent immediately sank out of sight, and Thor – wrathful at Hymer's interference – struck the giant such a blow that he tumbled headlong into the sea. In a moment, however, he had scrambled back into the boat, and bade Thor take up the oars and row back to land. When they reached the shore, Hymer

slung the two whales over his shoulder, and carried them up to his castle. Thor, having no fish, picked up the boat, and brought it along with him.

As soon as they were seated again by the fire, Hymer challenged his guest to prove his great strength by breaking a certain drinking-cup. Thor took the cup and threw it against the furthest stone pillar. It struck with a terrific crash, but – much to Thor's surprise – it fell to the ground unbroken. Then he hurled it at the massive granite wall, but it bounded back like a ball, and dropped at his feet. Thor looked very disconcerted as he stared at the uncracked surface of the cup; and, as he was about to own himself defeated, he heard a soft voice say, "Throw it at Hymer's head."

Though he knew that this kindly advice was given by Tyr's mother, he did not dare to turn and thank her, but he took up the cup and dashed it at Hymer's forehead. Terrific as the blow was, it did not seem to harm the giant at all, but the cup was shattered in a thousand pieces. The giant was very angry at having lost his wager; but he was now so thoroughly afraid of Thor's great strength and cunning that he made no objection when Tyr asked for the great kettle to carry back to the sea-god Aeger. "Take it then, if you must," he growled sullenly. Tyr made the first attempt to lift the kettle, but he could not so much as raise it from the ground. Thor, however, picked it up with great ease and set it on his head like a helmet. Then he marched boldly out of Hymer's castle with Tyr following close behind him.

They had not gone very far down the mountain when Tyr, looking back, cried out that they were being pursued. And true

enough, right at their heels was Hymer with a great company of giants ready to fall upon them. Thor did not even lift the kettle from his shoulders, but he swung the hammer around his head until the lightning flashed and the thunder shook the hills. Then he rushed at the giants, hurling the hammer right and left; and in a short time not one of the pursuers remained alive. Then Thor and Tyr resumed their journey, and soon came to the spot where the goat-chariot was waiting. This bore them swiftly to Aeger's palace, and the gods laughed merrily when they saw Thor enter with the kettle on his head. That night there was such a mighty brewing of ale that it seemed as if none of the company could ever be thirsty again.

8

THE BUILDING OF THE FORTRESS

Although the gods had felt less fear of the frost-giants since Mjölner the mighty hammer had been given to Thor, they were often very anxious when the Thunderer was obliged – as he sometimes was – to go off on a long journey. Then Asgard was left quite unprotected; for although the gods were brave and strong fighters, they would be no match for the frost-giants if their old enemies came against them in great numbers. So they wished very much for some assurance of safety in Thor's absence; and the best protection would undoubtedly be a high stone fortress that would encircle the whole of Asgard. But who was to build it?

Even if some of the gods were willing to undertake such a long, difficult task, who among them could spare the time for it, and who could lift the heavy stones that would be needed for the work? It seemed therefore as if the hope of having a fortress must be given up, for even Loki's quick wit could devise nothing; but one morning Heimdall, who guarded the rainbow bridge, blew

a loud blast on his horn to announce the approach of a stranger. When Odin looked down from his throne, he saw a huge figure standing beside Heimdall, and he knew at once that his visitor was one of the frost-giants. He stepped down from his golden throne, and, crossing the many-coloured Bifrost, he stood before the stranger.

"What do you seek here in sunny Asgard?" he asked.

"I am a master-builder," replied the giant, "and I have been told that you needed a clever mason to build you a fortress. Give me the work to do and you shall have a strong wall about your shining city."

Now Odin knew that no word about the proposed fortress had ever been breathed outside of Asgard; but he knew also that it was useless to make any denial, for the frost-giants, with their mysterious wisdom, had somehow learned the truth. So he said to the stranger: "We *do* need a fortress. Can you build one strong enough to resist any attack?"

"That I can," replied the giant, quickly. "And when my work is finished, I will promise you that all the forces in the universe could not move one stone from the wall."

"How long will it take you to build the fortress?" asked Odin.

"Just one year – which is a very short allowance of time for so great a task," answered the giant.

"And what payment do you ask for your work?"

"My wages must be the sun and moon and Freya for my wife," cried the giant, boldly.

This demand astonished and angered Odin; but, remembering how much he was in need of such help as the giant could give, he concealed his wrath under soft words and bade the master-builder come the next day for his answer.

When Odin called the gods together in the great council-hall and told them what the frost-giant demanded as payment for his work, a murmur of disapproval arose. Soon all the company cried out against making so dreadful a sacrifice; for it would be cruel to deliver the beautiful Freya to the arms of a giant. It was impossible to lose the maiden who was the light and joy of Asgard, and it was equally impossible to take the sun and moon from the heavens and compel the helpless earth to sit forever in darkness. So the gods decided to tell the giant that they would not accept his terms. Just then Loki spoke up.

"Let my wit and cunning – which you always condemn – find a way out of the difficulty. We will agree to the builder's demands, but you may trust me to see that he does not get a single one of the things he covets."

The gods were apt to doubt Loki's wisdom, and they always distrusted his motives; but they knew that his craftiness and trickery often helped him in his own difficulties, and they were now willing to use any means that offered a way out of their trouble. So they listened to Loki's plans, and next day, when the giant came for his answer, Odin told him that the gods would accept his terms if he would promise to build the fortress in a single winter. He was also to agree to give up his claims if the work was not finished by the first day of summer.

The giant was not pleased with these conditions, and he grumbled a great deal about the short time that was given him.

He promised, however, to undertake the building of the fortress, and agreed to have it finished by the first day of summer if he could have his horse to help him in his work. Now Loki was not present when the giant made this request; but Odin saw no reason why it should not be granted, so he told the builder to come the next day at sunrise and bring his horse with him. When Loki saw how the giant was going to be helped in the work, he was not so certain that his own wit could save the day; for the helper which the builder brought was an immense horse named Svadilfare, who could work night and day. This wonderful creature not only dragged the great blocks of stone for the building, but also set them in place with his strong fore-legs. The gods looked on in dismay as they saw how fast the work progressed, and berated Loki for having induced them to accept the giant's offer.

The long winter wore on, and the fortress grew as if by magic. The giant worked steadily without taking a moment to rest, and the wonderful Svadilfare brought pile after pile of huge stones to the spot where the builder was toiling with might and main. A few days before the end of the winter the work was all finished except one large slab that was to form the top of the gateway. The gods were now so alarmed at the prospect of having to pay the giant his extortionate wages that they threatened Loki with the direst punishments if he did not find some way out of the difficulty.

So that night as Svadilfare was wearily dragging to the gateway the last stone that was to complete the fortress, Loki changed himself into a pretty little mare; and, trotting up to the great horse, said – in perfect equine language – "Why must you work so hard when there are yet three days in which to lay this stone? Come with me for a romp in the meadows. You can be back again before your master returns."

Now Svadilfare knew that he ought not to leave his work; but his master was absent and he was very tired, and there was plenty of time to lay this last stone. So when the little mare trotted away still calling to him, he kicked off his harness and galloped delightedly after her. When the giant came to view the last of the work, one great stone lay by the unfinished gateway and the horse was nowhere to be seen. Believing that the gods had purposely hidden him in Asgard, he demanded the right to search the city; but no print of Svadilfare's feet were to be seen on the unmarred streets of gold. Then the giant rushed madly over the earth, and so heavy was his tread that the dwellers in Midgard awoke at night in terror, fearing that an earthquake was shaking the ground beneath them. Into the remotest corners of the earth and even as far as Jötunheim the giant searched for his missing horse; but he never found the secret grove where Loki was in hiding with Svadilfare. When the builder at last returned to Asgard, the first day of summer had dawned, and, by the terms of the agreement, he had forfeited his wages.

The gods had assembled just inside the fortress; and when the giant came raging toward them they were glad that Thor had returned from his long journey and now stood among them with the mighty Mjölner in his hand. The builder knew that in some way he had been tricked into losing his wager; so when Odin demanded that he should leave Asgard and not trouble the gods any further, he flew into a terrible rage and cried –

"If this fortress were not so strongly built, I would pull it to pieces so that you might not mock me." Then he rushed past the assembled company and into the many-pillared hall of Valhalla, crying:–

"Not for nothing does a frost-giant stand within the walls of Asgard. Your palaces are not built to stand forever, and I will send them crashing about your heads."

As he spoke, he grasped two of the pillars in his powerful arms, and it is probable that the beautiful building would have fallen if Thor had not rushed forward at this moment and struck the giant such a blow with his hammer that the builder's head was shattered into a thousand pieces. Then the huge body toppled headlong over the rainbow bridge, and kept on falling until at last it sank into the fathomless gulf that borders on the Land of Mists.

Thus the gods obtained their much-needed fortress, and Freya stayed happily in Asgard. There was now a sure protection against the invasion of the frost-giants; but over the gateway, one stone was always lacking, for no one among the gods was strong enough to set it into place.

9

HOW THE HAMMER
WAS LOST AND FOUND

The mighty hammer Mjölner was not only a protection to Asgard, but served to keep the frost-giants from doing harm to the earth. This whole race hated brightness, and were not content to live themselves in a land of ice and snow and mist, but tried to make all the world like their own dreary country. They longed to take the sunlight from the earth, to kill the flowers and cover every green thing with a mantle of blighting frost. They would have done all this if they had not been afraid of Thor's hammer, for whenever they strayed too far from Jötunheim and tried to nip the leaves and flowers with their icy fingers, Thor would drive them out of Midgard with his hammer; and the thunder and lightning would follow hard upon them until they were once more within the limits of their frozen hills.

One day Thor came back from a long journey, and being very

tired he dropped down on the steps of his palace and fell into a heavy sleep. When at length he awoke, he found to his horror and dismay that Mjölner was no longer in his hand or by his side. Some one must have come while he was sleeping and stolen it away. Thor felt certain that it was one of the frost-giants, for none of the gods, not even the mischief-loving Loki, would have dared to commit this theft. But no one had seen any of the giants lurking about Asgard, and Odin's ravens had not met with them in their flights to and from the earth. Yet it must have been some one of their ancient enemies who had stolen Mjölner, and therefore the hammer must be recovered speedily or the whole race of giants would soon come to take possession of Asgard now that its chief means of defence was gone. So Thor went in haste to Loki and begged him to devise some plan to recover the hammer.

"I will go myself," said Loki, "and see if I can find out who has stolen Mjölner. Perhaps we can regain it before it is too late, for the thief may not yet have spread the news of its capture to his kindred." Thor was ready to welcome any suggestion, so he readily agreed to this plan, and Loki hurried off to the flower-filled garden where Freya was wont to walk. He told the goddess of the theft of Mjölner and begged her to lend him her falcon plumage so that he might waste no time in his search. Freya gladly gave him her feathery disguise, and Loki sped northward across the frozen sea until he came to Jötunheim. He shivered continually under his delicate plumage, for this ice-bound land with its snow-covered mountains wrapped in the cold of eternal winter was different indeed from sunny Asgard.

He walked for a long time without meeting anyone, but at last he found the giant Thrym seated on the side of a mountain, counting his flock of sheep. The giant was very ugly, and he was also terribly big and strong, but Loki felt no fear of him. He perched on a rock beside Thrym, who looked at him craftily a moment and then said, "Why does Loki try to deceive those who know more than the gods?"

Seeing that his disguise would now be of little service, Loki assumed his own form, and drawing nearer to the giant greeted him in turn as a friend. Thrym did not seem at all surprised at seeing a god in Jötunheim; but he looked rather uneasily around, and went on counting his sheep without replying to Loki's greeting. The cunning god then instantly surmised that here was the thief who had taken Thor's hammer; so, in threatening tones, he accused the giant of the theft, and demanded that Mjölner be at once returned. It was a bold stroke, but it did not deceive Thrym in the least, for he knew that Loki was making mere empty threats, since Mjölner was no longer in Asgard.

Then Loki made the giant many promises of rich rewards from Odin, and told him of the good-will which all the gods would have for him if he returned the hammer to Thor. At this Thrym began to laugh, and he laughed so loud that the trees upon the mountain shook. Then he tore up by the roots a huge oak tree and threw it like a straw into the sea, and turning to Loki said: "You will never find that hammer, friend Loki, for I have buried it nine fathoms in the earth, and neither you nor Thor shall ever see it again. Yet, if you really need the hammer as a protection to your

city, there is one condition on which I return it. You must give me the beautiful Freya for my wife."

This proposal rather staggered Loki, for he knew how impossible such a thing was. But he said nothing, only bade Thrym good-by and hastened back to Asgard.

When Loki reported to Odin the result of his journey, the gods held a council to decide what it was best to do. Of course it was out of the question to try to induce Freya to become Thrym's wife, and Odin could not feel justified in demanding such a sacrifice. When the maiden herself learned of the giant's proposal, she grew so angry at the insult that the necklace of stars which she wore around her slender throat broke; and as the shining pieces fell through the air, people in Midgard exclaimed with delight at the shooting stars.

Since it was impossible to think of yielding Freya to a giant even to recover Mjölner, the gods tried to form some other plan, and again they turned to Loki for help, for he alone was clever enough to outwit the giant.

"There is no way to get the hammer," said Loki, "except by giving Thrym a bride; and since we cannot send any of the goddesses to the cold northland, we must find the giant another wife. Let us dress up Thor like a woman and send him instead."

"Never," roared Thor; "I should be the laughing-stock of everyone in Asgard."

"Nonsense," replied Loki, who rather enjoyed having Thor at his mercy; "and what if you were? Is that anything compared to seeing the whole race of frost-giants at the gates of Asgard? If something is not done very soon, they will be ruling here in our places."

The situation was indeed so critical that at length Thor consented to the plan, though much against his will. So Loki put on him a rich robe embroidered with gold, and wound a chain about his neck and put a beautiful girdle at his waist. Then he threw over Thor's head a long bridal-veil, while he attired himself as a waiting maid to attend the bride. The gods harnessed Thor's milk-white goats to the chariot, and together Thor and Loki set out for the frost-giants' country. It was very difficult to restrain the pretended bride from thrusting her sinewy hands from under the veil, and Loki feared that even a love-lorn giant would not be fooled into believing that those massive shoulders belonged to a maiden.

When Thrym beheld the bridal party coming, he was filled with joy and ran to meet them. He wished very much to raise the bride's veil, but Loki forbade him until after the wedding ceremony.

"The goddess Freya who has come to be your wife is very timid," said Loki, "and you must not distress her with your attentions, or she may grow frightened and wish to return to Asgard." So Thrym obeyed Loki's command, and led the bride to his palace, where his kinsmen were assembled. There they found the tables spread with meat and wine as if for a feast. Thrym urged his bride to partake of the fruits and delicacies which had been brought especially for her, and with some show of reluctance the supposed woman began to eat. First she devoured eight large salmon, then twelve roasted birds, and soon followed this up with eating a whole ox and drinking three barrels of mead.

"Did ever a maiden eat like this one?" thought the giants, and in their hearts they pitied Thrym for getting such a wife. When they spoke of the bride's appetite to Loki, he replied, "It is eight days since Freya has eaten anything, for she was so overjoyed at wedding Thrym, that she could not touch any food." Thrym was too happy to notice what the bride ate, and when the feast was over he cried to his brother, "Bring hither the hammer Mjölner and place it in the bride's lap; then let us be wedded in the name of Var."

So the hammer was brought and placed in Thor's hand; but the minute his fingers closed around it he tore the veil from his face, and the terrified giants beheld, not the mild countenance of Freya, but the face of the Thunderer himself. It was too late now to escape, and the giants were so frightened that they could not move, even if they had known where to flee from the fierce anger that blazed in Thor's eyes. He had barely swung the hammer twice around his head when thunder and lightning was mingled with the crash of falling buildings; and those of the giants who were not killed by the blows of the hammer were buried beneath the crumbling ruins. Thus did Mjölner return at last to Asgard.

10

IDUNA'S APPLES

Though sorrow sometimes came to the people of Asgard and they shared the burden of grief and trouble that afflicted the human race, as gods they had one privilege which belonged to them alone – the blessing of eternal youth. Sickness and old age never came within the gates of Asgard; and this was because the goddess Iduna had some very wonderful apples which gave, to those who ate of them, the strength and beauty of youth.

In appearance they were very much like other apples, of a beautiful red and gold; but when the gods had eaten of them they knew that such fruit could not be found anywhere outside of Asgard. For no other apples except those in Iduna's casket could bestow eternal youth and the power to defy all sickness and pain.

The goddess herself was very proud of her treasures, and proud, too, of the confidence which Odin placed in her in making her the guardian of a thing so priceless. The casket in which she kept the apples had only a single key, and this Iduna kept fastened to her

girdle. Wherever she went she carried the precious casket with her, and never let it be for a moment out of her sight. The gods felt no uneasiness while the apples were in such safe keeping, and there seemed to be no reason why they should ever lose the beauty and health and youth which had always been theirs. But one day both Iduna and her golden apples disappeared from Asgard, and no one knew where they had gone – no one but Loki, and he would not tell. This is how it happened.

Odin and Loki and Hoenir once went on a visit to the land of the frost-giants to find out, if possible, whether they were plotting any new invasion of Asgard. It was an uncomfortable journey, for the air was bitterly cold and the ground hard and frozen, so there was no pleasure in travelling. They even felt rather sorry for the people who were condemned to live forever in such a cheerless country. They were hungry, too, and could find nothing to eat; no game to kill, no fish to catch, not even any wild berries upon the barren hillsides. So Odin proposed that they return at once to Asgard; but just then Loki saw a herd of cows grazing near by, and exclaimed:–

"Here is meat in abundance. Let us eat before we set out again on our journey."

Then he killed the fattest of the cows, and bore it on his shoulder to the spot where Odin and Hoenir were already building a fire. They cut the meat and put it upon a spit; and while Loki turned it, the two others piled logs upon the fire. Now and then they tasted the flesh, thinking it must be cooked; but each time it was as raw as when they had first cut it. Then Odin threw on more logs, and the heat became so intense that the gods could hardly stand near it.

Still the meat remained uncooked. All night long they took turns cooking and tending the fire; but morning found them hungrier than ever, and with yet no prospect of a meal. This was too much for even the good-natured Hoenir, while Loki became so angry that he would have killed the whole herd of cows and thrown them into the sea out of mere spite. But Odin laughed and said:–

"Nay, Loki, do not let us vent our anger so foolishly. We will return, rather, to Asgard, and tell the gods that, in spite of the drink from Mimir's well, the frost-giants are yet wiser than Odin." For he knew that it was through some mysterious intervention of their old enemy that they could not enjoy the much-needed dinner.

Just then there came a loud noise and a whirring of wings overhead, and, looking up, they saw a large eagle hovering above them.

"Ha, ha," he cried, "so you cannot cook your dinner, I see. The meat must be tough indeed that will not yield to such a fire. But give me your promise that you will share the feast with me, and I will pledge you to get it cooked."

The gods promised very gladly, and the eagle, moving nearer, said –

"Stand aside and let me blow up the fire."

Suspecting nothing, the gods moved away, and as they did so the eagle swooped down, and, seizing in his strong claws all the meat that was on the spit, he began to flap his huge wings and rise slowly into the air.

When the gods saw that the eagle meant to trick them, they grew very angry, and Loki, hoping to snatch his prize from the treacherous giant – for that was what the thief really was –

grasped one end of the spit as it rose into the air and tried to drag it downward. But the eagle's strength was greater than the god's, and he flew higher and higher, carrying the luckless Loki with him. Up they soared, far above the heads of the bewildered Hoenir and Odin, who were helpless to rescue their comrade, and could only stand by and watch him disappearing from view. Over the frozen sea and the snow-covered mountains the eagle carried the unhappy Loki, not pausing in his flight until they reached a huge iceberg. Here he stopped, and dropped Loki upon the ground, where the bruised and weary god was glad to rest; for the eagle had dragged him over ice and snow, sharp stones and frost-bound stubble that stung like so many thorns.

The moment the bird alighted it was no longer an eagle, but the giant Thiassi, who grinned maliciously and said –

"How do you like flying, friend Loki?"

Loki was in such a rage that he was tempted to try to hurl the giant from the iceberg. He knew, however, that this would only shut him off from a speedy return to his companions, so he restrained his anger and said:–

"You can indeed rival the gods in swiftness, and I should be glad to journey farther with you, but Odin demands my return to Asgard. Take me back to him, therefore, with all speed."

The giant laughed at Loki's assumed boldness, and answered: "The gods are great indeed, but the frost-giants have no fear of them. Odin may need you in Asgard, but you shall not return except on one condition – that you promise to deliver into my power the goddess Iduna and her golden apples."

For some time Loki did not answer, for he hardly dared to make such a promise, since the loss of Iduna from Asgard would mean old age and possible death to the gods. Still, he did not intend to remain any longer on the iceberg. Knowing well the stubborn persistence of the whole race of giants, he felt that cajolery and threats were alike useless, so he said –

"I will promise."

The giant knew Loki's reputation for cunning, and therefore he demanded that the god should swear by Odin's spear to keep his promise. Loki did this, though with great reluctance, and the giant then assumed his eagle plumage and carried the god swiftly back to the place where Odin and Hoenir were still standing by the burnt-out fire. In answer to their questions, Loki told them of his strange journey, but made no mention of his promise to the giant. Then the three gods returned to Asgard.

Some time later, Loki went to the palace of Iduna and asked to see her apples. The goddess willingly brought out her casket, for she never wearied of looking at the precious fruit; but as she handed Loki the apples, she said –

"It is strange indeed for you to care so much for beauty – or is it that life is aging you more quickly than the others of Asgard, and you need still another of Iduna's apples?"

"Nay," replied Loki, "it is not for that reason that I desire to see your beautiful fruit; but because I wish to assure myself that they are really the best apples in the world."

"Why, where would you find such as these?" asked Iduna in surprise.

"Just beyond the gates of Asgard," answered Loki, "is a wonderful tree which bears fruit in all respects like these apples you prize so highly. I think they look even fresher, and as I tasted them I felt sure that they were finer in flavour than any you have here. It is a pity you cannot go and see them."

"Is it far from here?" asked the goddess, wistfully.

"No, indeed," replied Loki; "just outside the city gates. It would be such a delight to you to see them, for they are so fine as they hang in the sunlight, and so easy to reach, too. Some day I will tell you more about them, but now I must be away, for Odin has a commission for me today." So saying, he took his departure, and Iduna was left alone.

For a long time she thought over what Loki had said, and the longing grew very strong to go and see those apples which he had declared were even finer than her own. She dared not go away and leave her casket behind; but there surely could be no harm in taking it with her just a little way outside the gates of Asgard. Still she was doubtful and troubled, and wished that her husband, Bragi, were at home, that she might ask his advice. For a long time she hesitated, but at last her curiosity grew too strong to be resisted, and with her casket on her arm she left the palace and hurried outside the city gates.

She looked carefully all about her, but she saw no tree such as Loki had described. Discouraged and disappointed, she was about to return home, when she heard a loud noise overhead, and, looking up, saw a large eagle flying toward her. In a moment he had rushed down upon her, and before the terrified goddess realized

what had happened, he had caught her up in his strong claws, and was carrying her above the tree tops. In vain did she scream and struggle, for the eagle soared higher and higher, carrying her far out of sight of Asgard. He flew straight as an arrow across the mountains and over the frozen sea till he came to his home in the dreary northland. Here he took the form of the terrible giant Thiassi and began to beg the goddess for one of her apples. Iduna, frightened and trembling, kept the precious key of the casket clasped tight in her hand, and boldly refused to betray her trust by giving the giant even a sight of the apples. So Thiassi shut her up in his ice-walled palace and kept her there many days, not caring though she grew pale and sick with longing to return to sunny Asgard.

Meantime, the gods were greatly troubled at the sudden disappearance of Iduna; and her husband, Bragi, sought her, sorrowing, over all the earth. No one had seen her leave Asgard, and none knew where she had gone or when she would return – none save Loki, and he very wisely kept silent. At first the gods did not realize what the loss of Iduna and her apples meant to them; but as time went on and they felt weariness and old age creeping over them, they were filled with fear lest the goddess might never return, and there would be no longer any way to keep Death without the gates of Asgard. Odin's calm brow now became clouded, for not even his great wisdom was of any help in solving the mystery of Iduna's strange disappearance. The ravens, flying far and wide each day, brought no news of the missing goddess; and meanwhile Time was leaving its unwelcome marks on the faces

of the gods and goddesses. Frigga's hair began to turn white, and wrinkles furrowed the fair cheeks of Freya. The mighty Mjölner now trembled in the unsteady hand of Thor, and the feeble fingers of Bragi could no longer draw sweet music from his harp; in fact, all the dwellers in Asgard were growing old, and there was no way for them to renew their youth.

One day the ravens whispered to Odin that he should question Loki in regard to Iduna's disappearance, and Loki was summoned to appear before Odin's throne. When accused of knowing something of the missing goddess, he at first stoutly denied all knowledge of her; but Odin's look seemed to search his thoughts, and he saw that lying and deceit were of no avail. So he told all that he had done, and begged Odin's forgiveness. He promised to set out at once in search of the stolen goddess, and swore that he would not return to Asgard until he had found her and had brought Iduna and her apples safely home again. Once more he borrowed the falcon plumage of Freya and flew over to the frozen northland to the place where the giant kept Iduna a prisoner in his ice palace. He found her sitting alone and weeping bitterly; but Loki wasted no time in trying to comfort her. She was so overjoyed when the god assumed his own form and told her why he had come that she even forgave him for the misery he had led her into by his treachery. She said that fortunately Thiassi was off on his daily walk across the hills; but Loki, wishing to take all precautions, again put on his falcon plumage, and, by his magic arts, changed the goddess into a nut which he grasped firmly in his talons. Then, being warned by

Iduna that the giant never remained long away, he flew with her straight toward Asgard.

They had not gone far when Thiassi came home; and when he found Iduna gone, he knew that some of the gods must have come to her rescue. Nevertheless he determined not to lose her so easily; and taking the form of an eagle he flew high up into the air and looked about for some sign of the fugitive. Far in the distance he saw a moving speck among the clouds, and he followed quickly in pursuit. As he drew nearer he saw the falcon and its burden, and he knew that Iduna was being carried back to Asgard. So he redoubled his speed, and his great wings brought him rapidly nearer the falcon, whose laboured flight seemed to make an escape from the enemy impossible.

At Asgard the gods had assembled on the city walls, and they were now looking anxiously across the earth, fearing that some misfortune had overtaken Loki. At last they saw the falcon flying toward them, and they felt sure that this was Loki returning with his precious charge. But with the joy of this discovery came also a sudden fear as they saw the eagle following close behind the falcon, and seemingly in hot pursuit. These fears were confirmed as the birds drew nearer; and then the gods realized that if they would save Loki and Iduna, something must be done at once. Nearer and nearer came the falcon; but though his flight was swift, he could not keep the pace of his pursuer, and the eagle was steadily gaining on him. By this time the gods had built a great pile of wood on the city walls and were waiting until the falcon with his priceless burden had flown across it. The moment Loki passed, they quickly

set fire to the wood; and as the eagle came rushing blindly on, he flew directly over the flames, which caught his feathers and drew him down into the fire, burning him to death.

Iduna and her apples were safe at last in Asgard, and to celebrate her return Odin made a great feast in his palace hall, and the gods ate again of the golden fruit and became young and beautiful once more.

11

HOW THOR'S PRIDE WAS BROUGHT LOW: PART I

One morning Thor drove hurriedly out of Asgard in his chariot drawn by the milk-white goats, and set out on a wonderful journey. He did not tell Odin where he intended to go, for he knew that the All-Wise One would try to persuade him to give up the foolish expedition. For Thor's purpose was to travel all through Jötunheim until he met with the strongest of the giants, and then challenge him to a combat.

So he left Asgard secretly, and, avoiding the rainbow bridge as he always did when in his heavy-wheeled chariot, he directed his swift steeds toward Jötunheim. But though he passed through the gates of Asgard unseen by Odin, he was not quick enough for Loki, who, thinking that Thor's haste betokened some unusual

adventure, put on his magic shoes and followed the goats' flying feet. He found Thor quite willing to take him as a companion, and together the two gods hurried northward. They had hoped to reach Utgard, the great city of the giants, before night fell; but by the time they gained the shores of the ever-frozen sea that marks the boundary of Jötunheim, they found that it was too dark to travel any farther. So they looked about for some place to pass the night, and just over the hill they saw a small hut with a friendly light streaming from the window. When they asked here for food and shelter, the cottager gladly offered them a lodging for the night, but he confessed, reluctantly, that he had no food to give them.

"That trouble is soon remedied," cried Thor; and stepping over to where his goats stood browsing on the scanty grass, he struck them dead with one blow of his hammer. Then to the great surprise of the peasant and his family, he skinned the goats and spread their hides carefully upon the ground. After this was done, he offered their bodies to his host, saying: "Here is meat enough to furnish us with a bountiful dinner. I must beg of you, however, not to break a single one of the animals' bones, but throw them all on the goatskins."

The peasant and his wife carefully obeyed Thor's instructions, but the son, Thialfi, was so eager to get at the marrow in his bone that he broke it. This greedy act was not seen, however, so the boy hoped that no harm would come from his disobedience. The next morning when the gods made ready to resume their journey, Thor struck the goatskins with his hammer, and immediately the bones leaped into place. In a moment the two animals stood alive and whole before the eyes of the astonished cottagers; but one of the goats limped badly. When Thor noticed this he knew that his commands had been disobeyed, and he questioned the peasants angrily. He looked so terrible in his wrath that poor Thialfi did not dare to confess that he had broken the bone; and it was only when Thor threatened to kill the whole family if the guilt were not acknowledged, that the boy, terrified and trembling, admitted his deed.

As he seemed so truly sorry for what he had done, Thor relented and offered to take the lad with him as his servant. So, leaving the goats and the chariot in care of the peasant, the two gods resumed their journey. It was impossible to go very fast on foot, as the ground was frozen hard and covered with sharp bits of ice that cut through the travellers' light sandals. The difficulty in crossing the river was increased by the strong wind which blew from the high, bleak hills of Jötunheim, and seemed to lay an icy hand upon them.

So it was well on into the night before Thor and Loki reached a desolate stretch of moorland with mountains standing like grim sentinels all around it. This was the very heart of the frost-giants' country. There was no protection here that promised a night's rest, so the travellers kept on till they came to a strange building which, in the darkness, seemed to be a five-doored house, opening into a large courtyard. Here the gods built a fire to cook their evening meal, and then went gladly to bed, each of them taking one of the long, narrow rooms.

They had just fallen asleep when a great noise like the roaring of an angry sea filled their ears, and this was accompanied by a sort of trembling in the ground beneath them. Thinking it was a sudden earthquake, they waited for it to subside; but the rumbling only increased, and the strange noise grew almost deafening. This continued for hours, so that the travellers gave up all hope of sleeping, and at sunrise they set off again on their journey, after eating a hasty and sullen meal.

Their road now lay through the thick woods, and here they were soon halted by the sight of a giant stretched full length upon the ground. He was so big that even Thor and Loki, accustomed as they were to the size of the frost-giants, stared at him in surprise. As for Thialfi, he dropped the bag of provisions he was carrying, and hid behind a tree. The mystery of the strange noise was now solved, for the gods saw that it was merely the giant's snoring. The trees around him shook with his tremendous breathing, and the hills re-echoed to the deafening roar.

The sight of the giant sleeping so peacefully aroused Thor's anger, and he determined not to be disturbed any longer by the prodigious snoring. So he raised his hammer to strike a well-aimed blow at the sleeper; but just then the giant awoke. He sat up, and, smiling good-naturedly at the travellers, said, "What brings the mighty Thor and cunning Loki so far from Asgard?"

As it would be useless to try and deceive anyone as wise as a frost-giant, Thor replied: "I have come to Jötunheim to measure my strength against the mightiest of your people. Will you show us the way to the city of Utgard?"

"That I will do very gladly," cried the giant, getting up from the ground and stretching his huge body until it seemed as if his hands would touch the clouds. He then picked up a large sack that was lying near by, and throwing it over his shoulders, bade Thor and Loki follow him. Before they had gone far, he stopped, saying, "I have forgotten my glove; it must be somewhere in the forest." As he refused to proceed any further until it was found, the gods and Thialfi helped him in his search. Suddenly the giant reached over the tops of the trees, and picking up the very house in which the travellers had spent the night, exclaimed, "Here is my glove! I must have dropped it just before I went to sleep."

Putting the glove into his capacious pocket, and throwing his bag of provisions again upon his back, the giant started off across the hills. The gods had great difficulty in keeping within sight of him; and Thialfi, who was a swift runner, could barely hold to the pace the giant set as he covered mile after mile with each of his great strides.

At nightfall they were still far from the city of Utgard, so the giant proposed that they should eat their evening meal, and then sleep under the trees. The dinner was soon disposed of, and after the giant had eaten two roasted sheep and drunk a keg of ale, he stretched himself full length upon the ground. In a moment he was fast asleep and snoring louder than ever before.

The two gods knew that it was no use for them to think of sleeping, so Thor, having nothing better to do, laid hold of the giant's sack and tried to unfasten the string with which it seemed so loosely tied. But the more he pulled at it, the tighter drew the

cord, and Thor despaired of seeing what was inside the sack unless he ripped it open. This failure made him very angry, and his anger was further increased by the giant's continued snoring. When the gods wished to speak to each other, they could barely hear their voices above the thunder of the giant's snores.

At last Thor could restrain his wrath no longer; and, raising Mjölner high above his head, he dealt the sleeping figure a terrific blow. The giant opened his eyes, and looked slowly around him. "Did a leaf fall on my head?" he asked. "I thought that I felt something touch me." Then he went off to sleep again, and began to snore so heavily that the gods felt the ground shaking beneath them.

Thor was surprised at the ill-success of his blow, and he grew angrier than ever at the sight of the giant peacefully sleeping. Then he looked at the sack with its seemingly simple cord which he could not untie, and his wrath blazed out afresh. He rushed at the giant like a charging bull, and the blow which he dealt him made such a noise that for a moment it drowned the thunderous snoring. The giant roused himself with a shake and called, "Is anyone throwing acorns at me, or did a twig fall on my head?"

On receiving no answer to his question, he sat up, and looking around at Thor he smiled pleasantly and said: "Why are you not sleeping, my friends? If you do not rest, you will be too tired for your journey tomorrow. But perhaps you are still hungry; so take what you wish from my sack. There is plenty for us all." He tossed his bag of provisions nearer to the gods – then lay down again and went to sleep.

Thor was so furious by this time that he could barely wait until the giant was asleep before he grasped Mjölner in both hands and hurled it at the giant's head. Thialfi, seeing the god beside himself with rage, shrank back in fear before the terrible wrath that blazed in the Thunderer's eyes; and he hid his face in his hands when he heard the crash that shook the forest when Mjölner sank almost up to the handle in the giant's forehead.

The sleeper stirred uneasily, then sat up, looking first at the travellers, then up at the trees. "Are there any birds about here?" he asked. "I thought I felt one pecking at my forehead." Then he sprang to his feet, and, taking up his sack of provisions, he opened the bag very easily and took out half an ox. "It is almost daylight, and we must have an early start if we wish to reach Utgard by midday," he continued, smiling pleasantly at his companions, and offering them the contents of his sack.

Thor was so angry that he could not eat, but Loki and Thialfi made a good breakfast, and as they ate, the giant told them what they might expect when they reached the city of Utgard. "You may think that I am a fairly big fellow," he said, "but when you see those who live at the court of the king, you will consider me but a puny thing to be called a giant. If Thor wishes to find a worthy opponent, he will meet his equal among Utgard-Loke's men."

When the giant finished eating, he shouldered his sack, and laid on top of it the bag of provisions that the two gods had brought, hoping thus to lighten their travelling. Then he struck off on a rough path across the hills, with Thor and Loki hurrying after him, and Thialfi running at his heels. Soon they came within

sight of Utgard, and when they reached the city gates, the giant said: "I must leave you now, for my way lies in another direction. I think you will find a kindly welcome at the court of our king, and you need have no fear of coming to any harm, for the frost-giants respect the rights of a guest even if it is their ancient enemy. But I advise Thor not to boast too loudly of his strength until he is sure that his pride will not be humbled."

This last remark made Thor very angry, and his fingers closed tightly upon Mjölner; but he wisely kept his temper. He paid no heed to the friendly words of caution which the giant added as he said good-by, but strode on ahead through the great gates that guarded the city of Utgard.

12

HOW THOR'S PRIDE WAS BROUGHT LOW: PART II

The way to the palace was quickly found, and here the two gods were welcomed by the king. Utgard-Loke sat upon a lordly throne, surrounded by a company of giants so much larger than the others of this race which had from time to time made threatening visits to Asgard that Thor felt glad of the possession of Mjölner. When the travellers entered his halls, the king greeted them kindly and asked the object of their journey. Thor told him boldly that he had come to measure his strength against that of the giants, and Utgard-Loke courteously replied: "We have heard many tales of the might of Thor, the defender of Asgard; but we hope to show him that the frost-giants are no unworthy opponents. Before we begin our tests of strength, however, I will ask one of our youths

to meet your servant in some game of skill. Do you choose what it shall be?"

Now Thor knew that Thialfi was a very swift runner, so he answered that his servant would run a race with anyone of the king's young men. Utgard-Loke then called to a tall, slender youth named Hugi, and bade him make ready for the race. The company adjourned to an open meadow, and here the runners met to test their skill. Thialfi shot over the ground like an arrow sent by the practised bowman; but Hugi quickly outdistanced him and came first to the goal.

The gods were surprised and angry at the ease with which Hugi gained the victory; but when the king asked to have a second race, Thor eagerly agreed, and again Thialfi ran his swiftest. But although he flew with the lightness and speed of a race-horse, he found Hugi waiting for him at the end of the course.

Then Utgard-Loke said, "You are a good runner, Thialfi, but you need to put more speed in your feet before you can rival Hugi." Now Thor's servant was almost breathless from his running, and he was also very tired; but the king's tone seemed so insulting that he insisted upon a third trial. Again the two contestants ran over the course, but this time Hugi gave Thialfi the start of half a mile. In spite of this advantage, however, the young giant passed his competitor like the rush of the wind, and Thialfi lost the race a third time.

As the company had had enough of racing, they returned to the palace; and Thor, feeling angry and ashamed at his servant's defeat, began to wish he had never come to Jötunheim. Then

Utgard-Loke asked his guests if either of them cared to challenge one of his men at an eating contest, and Loki eagerly accepted this chance to prove his ability. "I can eat more than any two of this company," he cried boastfully, and gave a loud laugh of scorn when an immense trough full of meat was brought into the room and placed before him. Then the king summoned Logi to contend with the brother of Odin, and he and Loki sat one at each end of the trough.

There was surely never such eating seen before in all the world. Loki devoured the food so fast that it seemed as if he would finish all that was set before him in less than a minute; but when he came to the middle of the great dish, he found that Logi had not only eaten his own share, but had finished up the meat and bones and trough all together.

"Now let us see what the mightiest of the gods can do," said the king, as Loki withdrew to the furthest end of the hall. Thor had been looking on gloomily at Loki's failure; but the king's tone roused up all his anger, and he stepped boldly forward, saying, "I will undertake to empty in one draught any drinking horn that you can place before me." So Utgard-Loke commanded his men to bring out a great drinking horn, and as he handed it to Thor the king said: "Here is a cup which the youngest among us can empty in three draughts. A strong man needs to quaff it twice, but a mighty warrior such as you should finish it all at one drinking." The king's tone was so insulting that Thor felt his fingers tighten on the handle of his hammer, and he longed to hurl it at Utgard-Loke's head; but he took the horn and set it to his lips.

He drank long and deeply until he felt sure that he had drained every drop of the liquid; but when he looked into the horn, he saw that it was but half emptied. "What is the trouble, is the drink too large for the Mighty One of Asgard?" asked Utgard-Loke, contemptuously. At these words Thor flew into a great rage, and, grasping the horn more tightly, he drank as he had never drunk before. Then he set the vessel down, feeling sure that it must now be empty; but he found to his surprise that it was hardly less full than before he began to drink. A loud laugh of derision greeted him, and the king cried scornfully: "Is this the great skill in drinking of which you boasted so freely? The emptying of this horn should be but child's play; but perhaps the mighty Thor is weary."

"Give me the horn," roared the angry god, who was raging inwardly at having to endure these taunts. So a third time Thor drank; and when he stopped to take breath, he threw the horn aside, not waiting to look down into it, for he felt certain that there could not be a drop left in it. But one of the giants caught it up and showed him how much of the liquid still remained. Enraged at this unexpected humiliation, Thor refused to drink any longer, and would barely listen when Utgard-Loke asked him if he would engage in any trial of strength. "We will propose a game which is a favourite pastime among our children, so the defender of Asgard will be able to do the thing with ease. It is merely to lift my cat from the ground."

These words so infuriated Thor that he strode angrily out of the hall, but before he had gone far, he encountered a huge bunch of bristling fur that effectively barred his way. His first impulse was to strike the cat with his hammer, but remembering Utgard-Loke's insulting words, he grasped the great creature by the middle, intending to throw it aside. But though he tried with all the strength of his powerful arm to move the cat, he could not stir it from its place; and the higher he sought to lift it, the higher it arched its back without ever raising one foot from the ground. Thor's arm was now lifted as high as it would go, but he could not budge the great cat an inch. So at last he let go his hold and turned to meet the scornful laughter of the whole company of giants.

"Is this the strength we have been taught to fear?" cried Utgard-Loke. "Surely the gods do not call so puny a fellow as this the defender of Asgard. Perhaps Thor is only mocking us, however, and will prove his boasted strength in some worthier contest."

"Give me a chance to wrestle with the strongest giant among you, and I will soon show you whether my strength can be scorned!" cried Thor, who was longing to hurl his hammer at the king's head and make him cease his insulting words.

"Your boasting has all been idle," said Utgard-Loke, looking sternly at the angry god, "so I will not match you against our strongest men. But here comes my old nurse, Ellie, and you may try a wrestle with her."

Thor looked around as a shrivelled old woman, bent and toothless, hobbled feebly into the hall. Her sightless eyes seemed to blink with an almost supernatural intelligence as she made her way straight toward the spot where the god was standing. "Do not

scorn to wrestle with old Ellie," cried the king, "for she has got the better of many a strong man before now."

So Thor grasped the hag firmly and tried to throw her to the ground, but she gripped his body with her thin arms and clung to him with such amazing strength that he had to exert all his force to keep from being strangled. The more he struggled, the tighter grew the old woman's hold, and even his arm which held the hammer was rendered useless by her vice-like grip. He felt himself slowly weakening, and soon one knee was on the ground. Then the hag loosed her hold, and, with a mocking laugh, hobbled out of the hall.

Thor rose up, ashamed and humiliated by this last defeat; but the anger had died out of his eyes, and he stood before Utgard-Loke with bent head. No one had ever seen the strongest of the gods so humbled. Then the king smiled upon him kindly and said, "Let us forget both our pride and our foolish boasting, and share the feast as friends; for we will now offer you the best of food and drink that there is in the land of Jötunheim." So a bountiful meal was spread before them; and, in the friendly hospitality of the king, Thor forgot the insults which he had lately received at Utgard-Loke's hands.

The next morning the king accompanied his guests to the gates of the city; and when they were well outside the walls he said to Thor: "Now that you are no longer within our gates, I will confess to you that during your brief stay among us, we have been not only amazed but terrified at seeing how great indeed is your strength. We know now that all our combined forces would have been powerless against you unless we had deceived you by our magic arts. For it was not superior skill or strength that defeated you in the contests, but enchantment. It was I whom you met in the forest, and when I found how terrible was Thor's strength, I knew that it was rash to admit such a foe within our gates unless he could be deceived by magic, and his strength be met by cunning. I tied the sack with a cord that no one but myself could possibly undo, for every knot was made under a magic spell. Each time you struck me those terrific blows, I quickly slid a mountain between myself and the hammer; and you may now see the deep clefts which those blows have made. When Thialfi ran with Hugi, it was against Thought that he was racing; and when Loki strove with Logi, his opponent was none other than Fire, who consumes whatever he touches. You took such deep draughts from the horn that we were all amazed at your wonderful drinking; but the other end of the horn was in the sea, so try as you would you could never drain it dry. You will notice, however, as you look over the earth, that the level of the ocean has fallen far beyond its lowest ebb-line, owing to your enormous drinking. The cat which could not be raised from the ground was really the Midgard serpent, and we giants trembled, indeed, when we saw how high you lifted it. Lastly the old nurse, Ellie, whose strength seemed so marvellous to you, was not a woman, but Old Age itself; and in her hold even the greatest warrior is bound to weaken and fall."

When Thor heard these words of Utgard-Loke's, he was so furious at the trickery that had been put upon him that he rushed at the speaker with upraised hammer. But before the blow could

fall, the giant had disappeared; and when Thor looked about him he no longer saw the gates of Utgard nor any sight of the great city. He and Loki were standing on one of the bleak moorlands over which the winds of Jötunheim blew forever night and day.

13

THE WOOING OF GERD

The god Freyr was busy enough in the summertime when the sun shone upon the earth and everything bloomed and blossomed under his untiring care; but when winter came there was no work for him to do in orchards or meadows, and he grew restless from the long enforced idleness. So one day when Odin was away on some necessary journey, Freyr strolled idly through the golden streets of Asgard, and wished that he might sometime be taken as a companion when Odin went wandering among the dwellings of men. He wondered whether there was any spot in Asgard from which he could look down and see what was going on in the earth, and the longing grew very strong to see where Odin had gone.

There was one place which commanded a view of all the world, but Freyr did not dare to think of usurping it, for Odin's throne was held so sacred that no other god had ever ventured to set foot there. Dismissing this thought from his mind, Freyr

wandered restlessly about from one marble hall to another, but getting nearer each moment to the great gold throne, until at last he stood directly before it. A long time he hesitated, thinking of the punishment that might fall upon him if Odin suddenly returned; but finally the desire to see all the kingdoms of the earth grew too strong to be resisted, and Freyr boldly stepped into Odin's sacred seat.

He gave a gasp of wonder and delight as his eyes travelled quickly over the wonderful panorama of earth and sky that lay spread out before him. Far away to the north stretched ice-encircled Jötunheim, whose snow-capped mountains reached up into the clouds. Still farther away lay the Land of Mists with its chill fogs, reaching out toward Muspelheim. The earth itself, which Freyr knew so well, looked wonderfully fresh and new when seen from this exalted place; and he felt that he himself would never weary of watching over the affairs of men, if only he could occupy Odin's seat.

He did not care to rest his gaze very long on frozen Jötunheim, for there was nothing in that dreary country to attract the beauty-loving Freyr; but as he chanced to look at a tall old castle standing on the top of one of the wind-swept hills, he saw the door suddenly open. Then a maiden appeared on the threshold, and Freyr gazed upon her with surprise and delight, for she seemed too beautiful to belong to the grim race of giants.

She stood a moment in the doorway, a very embodiment of warmth and youth and light; and when the doors at length closed behind her, Freyr felt that all the brightness had gone out of the world. Never before had he seen any maiden whom he wished to make his wife; but here in the land of the frost-giants he had found one whose loveliness already made him thrill at the mere thought of her.

He descended slowly and sadly from Odin's throne, and began to wander aimlessly about Asgard, more restless and unhappy than before he had taken that unfortunate glance toward Jötunheim. For many days he roamed through the marble-pillared halls, seeking some distraction to make him forget the golden-haired maiden whom he loved; but always his thoughts turned toward the castle on the wind-swept hill, and he longed – till he grew sick with longing – for a sight of the giant's daughter.

One day his trusted servant Skirner asked him why he looked so sad; so Freyr told him of his longing for the golden-haired maiden, and of how he had watched her from Odin's throne. Then Skirner offered to make the journey into Jötunheim at once, and do his best to woo the giant's daughter for his master. So Freyr gave him his swiftest horse, and filled his hands with rich gifts, and finally girded upon Skirner his own sword, which he promised to give to the wearer if the mission should be successful. Then he bade Skirner ride with all speed northward.

As fast as the faithful horse could carry him, Skirner hurried toward the giants' country; and when the setting sun threw the long, black shadows of the hills across the snow-covered ground, he crossed the last of the fiords that lay at the edge of Jötunheim. Then a short, hard gallop over the frozen ground brought him to the foot of the castle where the giant Gymer lived with his beautiful daughter. As he neared the gates, two enormous dogs

sprang at him, barking furiously; and it was with difficulty that Skirner guided his horse well out of their reach. Not far away was a shepherd leading his flock to the scanty pasturage; and Skirner, riding slowly up to him, asked how he might be able to enter the castle.

"What do you seek here?" inquired the shepherd. "No stranger ever comes to Gymer's hall."

"I wish to speak with the giant's daughter," replied Skirner.

The shepherd shook his head. "It is safer to have speech with Gymer than with the beautiful Gerd," he said. Then, looking kindly at the horse and rider, he added, "If you are wise, you will not go too near the castle gates, but call aloud her name, and perchance she may come to answer you."

So Skirner called loudly to the maiden until the hills re-echoed to the name of Gerd; and the giant's daughter listened to the cry, wondering who the stranger might be that would dare to use her name thus boldly.

Angry, and yet curious to see who stood without the castle, Gerd threw open the great hall doors; and at the sight of her the two fierce dogs stopped howling and lay quiet at her feet. Then Skirner came boldly to the maiden's side and begged her to listen to his story. As the laws of hospitality prevailed even in Jötunheim, the beautiful Gerd bade him enter; and when they were seated by a great fire in the hall, Skirner told the maiden how Freyr had seen her from Odin's seat and had loved her with a passion that would surely kill the once-joyous god unless she consented to become his wife.

Gerd listened coldly to the speaker's words, and his impassioned pleading left her unmoved. When Skirner finally spoke of taking her at once with him to Asgard, she cried angrily, "Go back to your master and tell him that though he should die for love of me, Gymer's daughter will never wed with one who is the enemy of her race."

Then Skirner brought out a wonderful ring and many costly gems – the gift of Freyr – and offered them to Gerd; but she haughtily refused to touch them.

"You cannot tempt the daughter of Gymer with gold," she said. "I have plenty here in my father's palace."

Failing in this, Skirner drew his sword – the coveted blade which he hoped to win for himself by the success of his mission – and flashing this before the maiden's eyes he swore by the spear of Odin that he would kill her if she would not consent to wed with Freyr. But Gerd only laughed at his threats, and looked unmoved at the glistening steel.

"Keep your sword to terrify mortal maidens, or those who sit spinning in the halls of Asgard. The daughter of Gymer knows no such thing as fear," she said.

As neither gold nor threats could move the beautiful Gerd to listen to his master's suit, Skirner tried his last resource; and, calling upon all the powers of earth and air and water, he pronounced a terrible curse upon the maiden for her coldness to the unhappy Freyr. "May the sun never shine without bringing pestilence upon your land, and may each day add some trouble to those which already burden you. May sickness throw its blight upon you, and

loathsome diseases render your beauty hideous. May old age lay its hand on you before youth is over, and may you sit lonely and desolate among your barren hills. May all the good things of life turn to gnawing pains until you are glad to pray for death. So shall there be no peace for you in all the world for having spurned the love of Freyr."

At first the maiden paid no heed to these fearful words; but soon they seemed to weave a sort of magic spell about her. She trembled, and her beautiful face grew pale with fear. Suddenly she stretched out both white arms to Skirner, crying, "Does Freyr indeed love me so deeply that he can invoke all the powers of the earth to curse me for not wedding him?" Then Skirner told her how great his master was, and how truly the curse would be fulfilled if she hardened her heart against the love of Freyr. And as she listened to the speaker's eager words of praise, the heart of Gerd was touched and she gave Skirner her promise to become Freyr's wife.

"Though," she added sadly, "it is strange indeed for Gymer's daughter to wed with a god." Skirner tried to persuade her to return with him at once to Asgard, but she said, "Go back to your master and tell him that I will meet him nine days hence in the groves of Bar-isle."

So Skirner mounted his horse again and rode away from Jötunheim. Though the journey back to Asgard was as long and hard as his coming had been, it seemed to him to be far less wearisome; for the horse shared his rider's gladness and galloped more lightly over the frozen ground, and the woods looked no longer as if peopled with dreadful shapes and shadows. When Skirner neared Asgard he saw far in the distance Freyr standing by the rainbow bridge eagerly watching for his messenger's return. The impatient god did not wait, however, until horse and rider came close enough for him to see the gladness on Skirner's face; but, believing that his servant had been unsuccessful, since he rode alone, Freyr turned sadly away. He did not even wish to speak with the man who had done him so great a service; but thought only of the loss of Gerd.

Then Skirner spurred his faithful horse till its hoofs struck fire from the hard stones beneath; and when the gates of Asgard were reached, he rushed eagerly in search of Freyr to tell him of Gerd's promise. The god's face was lit with a great joy as he heard that his love was to be rewarded, and that Gymer's beautiful daughter was willing to become his wife.

The nine days of waiting seemed very long to the impatient lover; but at last the time came when the sun shone as it had never shone before, the trees blossomed – although it was still winter – and flowers bloomed along the path that led to the groves of Bar-isle. Then Freyr, full of the glad spirit of youth and love and springtime, went gayly to the trysting place; and there beneath the newly leafing trees stood Gerd, more beautiful by far than when he had seen her standing in her father's halls.

14

HOW THOR FOUGHT THE GIANT HRUNGNER

One day Odin took a long journey into a land far beyond the seas; and as his road homeward lay through Jötunheim, he went with all speed across that dreary country. With the swiftness of the wind his wonderful horse Sleipnir carried him over the ice and snow that lay thick on the frozen ground; and sometimes, when the mountains loomed very tall in front of them, the horse rose into the air, soaring through mist and cloud as easily as some great bird.

Then as the golden hoofs of Sleipnir struck fire from the hard rocks that seemed to spring up everywhere beneath his feet, Odin rejoiced in the strength and beauty of his horse, for he knew that there was not its like in all the world. He had almost crossed the last stretch of treeless country on the edge of Jötunheim, when he

saw a giant seated on a rock, with his horse standing idly beside him. As Sleipnir came rushing by, the giant called out: "Ho! stranger. Why do you ride so swiftly?"

Odin drew rein and came back to the rock where the speaker sat. The giant looked critically at Sleipnir's splendid head and arching neck; then he said, "That is a fine horse you have."

"There is no steed that can equal him in beauty or in swiftness," replied Odin, proudly. The giant scowled at these boastful words, and replied angrily:–

"Not so fast, my friend. It is easier to talk than to prove the truth of one's words. Now my horse Goldfax is fully as fine as yours; and there is nothing to match him for speed in the whole land of Jötunheim."

"Jötunheim!" cried Odin, contemptuously. "What could you expect from such a country as this? Why, my steed was reared in the sunny meadows of Asgard, where he still pastures night and day."

"Well, whatever he is, there is no need for us to waste words in boasting," said the giant. "Let us run a race and prove whose horse is the better."

Odin gladly agreed to this; and when the giant mounted his horse Goldfax, the two riders set off on a gallop that made the hills re-echo to the sound of clattering hoofs. Sleipnir, overjoyed at the prospect of a race with something worth his mettle, threw back his head and sped like an arrow toward Asgard. The giant followed close behind, and so full was he of the excitement of the chase that he was unaware of being carried within his enemy's gates. Heimdall, who stood watching by the rainbow bridge, looked on in surprise as the Ruler of Asgard rushed swiftly by; and he would have sounded the usual alarm at the sight of the giant following, if Odin had not signalled to him to let the strange horse and rider go past.

When the giant, whose name was Hrungner, found himself surrounded by so many of those who were his sworn enemies, he grew fearful and began to look helplessly about him. Soon he realized, however, that the laws of hospitality assured every kindness to a guest, and he knew that he was as safe in Asgard as he would be in Jötunheim. So when Odin summoned him to the feast at Valhalla, Hrungner sat down to eat and drink with the gods, feeling at heart very proud to be in the midst of so noble a company.

As the feast progressed, and the giant drained one horn after another of the sparkling drink the gods supplied, he began to grow boastful. He laughed at the smallness of Odin's shield-hung hall, and told of the great palaces that were built by the frost-giants. He boasted loudly of his own great strength; and as he drank more and more of the wine so freely poured, he cried: "What a puny lot of men you are to call yourselves gods! There is not a giant in Jötunheim who could not beat anyone of you in single combat. If I chose to make so unfair a return for your hospitality, I could pull this poor little hall about your ears, and not leave one stone upon another in the whole of Asgard."

The gods grew very angry at these insulting words; but as Hrungner was their guest, they could not punish him as he

deserved. So the giant continued drinking; and as his swaggering grew more unbearable, the gods with difficulty restrained themselves from striking him dead where he sat. "I shall drink every drop of wine in Asgard before I leave here," he cried, glaring drunkenly at Odin. "Then I shall pick up a handful of you people that are called gods, and carry you off to Jötunheim as playthings for my children."

So pleased was the giant with his own wit that he began to laugh until the cups rattled upon the table. The gods felt they could not endure his presence any longer, and determined to hurl him out of Asgard, even if he was their guest. But Loki, who was enjoying the giant's boasts and drunken wit, begged them not to act too hastily; so Hrungner kept on drinking unmolested. Suddenly he threw his cup with a crash to the ground, and, looking insolently around at the company, cried, "The gods have always been the enemies of the frost-giants; but soon I will drive them from their lofty place, and take Sif and Freya to be my servants."

This insulting speech was more than the gods could bear; so they called upon Thor to rid them of the braggart in any way he desired. Then Hrungner saw the wrathful face of the god approaching, and saw, too, the upraised hammer; but he was too full of drunken courage to feel afraid. Before Mjölner fell, he roared savagely at Thor: "If I had my shield and flintstone here, you would not dare to come at me with your wonderful hammer. It is very brave of you to strike an unprotected guest."

At these words Thor's arm dropped to his side, and the giant gave a mocking laugh.

"Let this mighty fighter meet me in single combat on the plains of Jötunheim, and then I will prove that the frost-giants are stronger than any of the timid dwellers in Asgard."

Thor was only too ready to accept the challenge, and arranged to meet the giant on a certain plain in Jötunheim. Then Hrungner, who felt that there was nothing more for him to do or say in Asgard, took his departure; and, returning to his own country, spread the news that there was to be a mighty combat between himself and Thor. The giants did not feel very certain of Hrungner's victory over the god, so they decided to help him in every possible way. They made a huge giant out of clay and stood him on the plain where the battle was to be fought, hoping by this stratagem to deceive Thor. As there was no human heart to put into the clay giant, they gave him a mare's heart, and this made the poor creature so timid that he could barely be induced to stand still on the plain and await Thor's coming.

Beside the newly made giant stood Hrungner with his shield and flintstone, secretly hoping that Thor would mistake the clay figure for that of his opponent, and so spend the first force of his blows on the mock giant's head. Suddenly on the crest of the mountain appeared a runner; and soon Thor's servant, Thialfi, came speeding toward them. He called loudly to Hrungner: "My master is on his way to meet you; but he will not follow on the road I came. He is coming along underground, and will attack you from beneath." The stupid giant believed this; so he threw his shield on the ground and stood firmly upon it, with the flintstone in his hand, ready to strike Thor's head the moment it emerged.

Soon there came a sudden roaring sound as if all the waters of the earth were rushing to pour themselves into the sea; the sky darkened, and through the thick clouds the lightning gleamed and flashed over the darkening plain. Nearer and nearer came the crashing of thunder which heralded Thor's approach, and the hills answered with long, deep peals. Then on the brow of the hill overlooking the plain appeared Thor's majestic figure, so terrible to behold that most of the giants fled away in fear. With incredible swiftness he rushed upon Hrungner, and the hammer – whirled through the air by his mighty arm – flew straight at the giant's head. The terrific force of the blow hurled Hrungner at once to the ground, but not before he had thrown his flintstone at Thor's forehead.

The noise of the combat was like the crashing of many mountains together. Hrungner fell to the ground like an oak tree that has received the last stroke of the axe; and, as he fell, Thialfi sprang at the clay giant and disposed of him with one straight blow. The flintstone which Hrungner had thrown, sank into Thor's forehead; and the sudden pain made him so dizzy that he staggered forward and fell just where Hrungner's great body lay stretched upon the ground. Then Thor found to his dismay that one of the giant's feet was resting firmly on his neck; and, try as he would, he could not get free. So he bade Thialfi bring his little Magne, who was only three days old, and when the child came, he easily lifted the great foot from his father's neck. Thor was very proud of this display of strength, and he wished to give his son the giant's horse Goldfax, but Odin would not permit the gift.

The frost-giants were discouraged over the complete defeat of their champion, but they took great satisfaction in seeing the flintstone which Hrungner had driven into Thor's forehead. When the Thunderer returned to Asgard he found that the stone caused him much pain, and there seemed to be no way to remove it. So he sent for the sorceress Groa, who, as soon as she came, began to weave her magic spells, and chant weird songs, and Thor felt the stone in his head already beginning to loosen. While Groa continued her incantations, and the pain in his head grew less and less each moment, Thor tried to think of some way in which he could reward his benefactress for her kindness. Orvandel, Groa's husband, had been for many years away from his home; and as the sorceress loved him very dearly, there was nothing she wished for so much as his return. Thor was partly responsible for her husband's disappearance, for Orvandel had once angered him so that he had put the offender into a basket and carried him to a far-off country, where he left the unfortunate man to find his way back alone. During the journey the air was so cold that poor Orvandel nearly perished in his narrow prison. As it was, one of his toes which protruded from the basket really did freeze; and this made Thor so ashamed of his harsh treatment of Orvandel that he set the prisoner free. Then he placed his toe in the sky as a star, and in the northern heavens there is a bright constellation which is still known as Orvandel's Toe.

When Thor told Groa what he had done, and promised to bring her husband back to her at once, the sorceress became so overjoyed at the prospect of Orvandel's return that she forgot

all her magic arts and spells. Full of happiness at the thought of seeing her husband, she suddenly stopped her weird singing, and was unable to resume it, though Thor begged her to continue the enchantment until the stone was loosed. But Groa had lost all her mystic power, and could never charm things from their place again. So the flintstone remained in Thor's forehead, and in the far-off countries of the north, the children are taught not to throw any stone too hard upon the floor, for when it strikes the ground the flint in Thor's forehead moves, and causes the god much pain.

15

THE STORY OF BALDER

In all the city of Asgard there was no god so beautiful or so dearly loved as Balder. Wherever he went it was like the coming of sunshine, and every grief fled away before the brightness of his presence. In all his happy life he had never known a moment's sadness, and the gods believed that none could ever come to him. So beautiful and joyous and free from care was Balder that he seemed to the gods to be the one among them who could surely never share in the final doom which they knew awaited all the dwellers in Asgard.

The days passed happily for Balder, and no thought of sorrow crossed his untroubled mind, until one night he had a dream which filled him with strange fear. When the gods met again in council he told them his dream, and begged them to interpret its meaning. They tried to laugh and banish his fears, but at heart they felt that an evil day had come. Over Asgard now hung a dark shadow which foreboded the coming sorrow, for the dream spoke

of approaching evil, even of death. So full of sadness did the gods become at the thought of losing Balder, that they cared no longer to join in their accustomed games or to make merry while some tragic fate might be overshadowing the bright and joyous youth.

Odin could not rest until he learned the truth about his favourite son; so he mounted Sleipnir and rode down to the dark region where the goddess Hel ruled over her innumerable dead. In those silent halls he found a table spread, and dishes of gold and silver were set out as if for some honoured guest. At the head of the table was one vacant seat; and when Odin saw this, his heart sank with fear, for he knew too well for whom the chair was waiting. Hoping against hope, in spite of this sinister sight, Odin returned to the earth and sought out a certain wood where a famous prophetess had long ago been buried. Over her grave he uttered some mystic words that roused the sleeper from her age-long rest, and at last she spoke in a faint, far-off voice. "Who is it that comes to break my sleep?"

And Odin answered, "I am Voltam, and I have come to ask why the table is so richly spread in Helheim and for whom the vacant chair stands waiting." Thus Odin spoke, for he feared to tell her his name.

A silence fell over the dim old forest, and for a moment Odin feared that his spells could not compel the dead to speak. But at last a faint voice whispered, "It is for the shining Balder that Hel and all her hosts are waiting."

"Who then shall send the Beloved of the gods to Helheim?" asked Odin, and he waited fearfully for the answer.

"Blind Höder shall slay him, for so it has been written, and so it shall be," came the words which the anxious listener dreaded and yet waited to hear.

"And who shall avenge the death of Balder?" he asked sorrowfully. For a long time no answer came; then the voice, which sounded still farther away, cried mournfully:–

"Keep me no longer from my well-earned rest. For ages upon ages I have lain here, and the rain and snow have beat upon my head and the winds have sung their songs in my ears. Depart thou hence and leave me to my sleep."

So Odin left the forest, for he knew that the dead would speak no more; and slowly and sorrowfully he returned to Asgard. He did not tell the gods of his visit to Helheim; but kept to himself the sad knowledge he had gained.

Meantime the goddess Frigga determined to avert, if possible, the unknown danger that threatened her son; so she went out one day from her palace and wandered over the whole earth. And as she went she begged everything which she met to swear by a solemn oath never to hurt Balder. Fire, water, rocks, trees, iron, brass, birds and beasts – all were bound by a vow to do no harm to him; and everything on earth gave the promise gladly, for all the world loved the bright and joyous Balder. As Frigga was returning home, she saw just outside the gates of Asgard a small plant called the mistletoe; but it looked so harmless that she passed it by without asking for the promise, and hurried on to tell Odin of the success of her journey.

When the gods heard how everything had sworn never to hurt

Balder, there was gladness again among them. But Odin, knowing the decree of the Norns, could not rejoice with the rest; though in the general happiness that reigned now in Asgard, no one marked his sadness. Then, to prove whether all the things which had given the promise would really keep their word to Frigga, the gods placed the youth as a target before them, and hurled at him huge stones and sharp-pointed spears and the weapons which they used in battle; but each missile turned aside, and refused to hurt the shining Balder. Even the deadly battle-axes fell harmless at his feet. Now Loki, who always hated everything beautiful, and who was jealous of Balder because the gods loved him, stood by watching the game. His heart was full of bitterness and envy, and he hated the glorious youth who could be so confident and secure in the love which all the world had owned for him. So he determined to work some harm to Balder.

One day a strange old woman came to the palace of Frigga and asked to have speech with her. The goddess was sitting with her maidens spinning, and when the old woman was admitted to her presence, she spoke to her kindly and asked the object of her visit.

"I have come, lady," said the old woman, who was really Loki in disguise, "to learn what is going on here in Asgard that the shouts of joy reach even to the earth. I hear laughter and cheering in the court where the gods are at their games. Tell me, what does it mean?" Then Frigga smiled happily and said, "It means that the gods are hurling their battle-axes at Balder and trying to wound him, but he stands before them unhurt, for everything on earth has sworn to me to do him no harm."

"Has everything indeed made you this promise?" asked Loki.

"Yes," answered Frigga; "everything except a little plant called the mistletoe, and this looked so small and weak that I did not ask it to promise."

"And does this mistletoe grow far from here?" continued the pretended old woman.

"Just at the gates of Asgard," answered Frigga. And Loki, having learned what he wished, left the palace exulting in the ease with which he had deceived the unsuspecting goddess. Laying aside his disguise, he sought the place where the mistletoe grew, and cutting off a branch, he shaped it into an arrow. Then he went to join the gods in their sport.

Just outside the circle of the players stood Höder, the brother of Balder, silent and alone, for he was blind and could not share in the games. Going up to him, Loki said –

"Why do you not join in the sport, Höder, and throw some missile at the wonderful Balder who now bears a charmed life?"

"Because I cannot see where he is standing," answered Höder, "and besides, I have no weapon to throw."

"If that is all," said Loki, "come with me and I will give you an arrow and help you shoot it." So he led Höder forward, and the blind god followed him willingly, for he dreamed of no evil.

Then Loki put the arrow into his hand and directed his aim so well that the fatal shaft flew straight to Balder's heart, and in a moment the beautiful god lay dead.

There was mourning now in Asgard, and over all the world. The sun no longer shone with its accustomed brightness; the birds

stopped their singing, and the flowers drooped their heads; even the beasts felt the sadness that lay upon the earth, and crouched silent in their dens. Everything that loved the shining Balder now wept and mourned for him. Then the gods arrayed his body in the finest cloth of gold, and brought it down to the sea, where Balder's ship lay close to the water's edge. Very sadly they laid the body upon its deck, and heaped around the beloved form rings and chains of finest gold, jewels and weapons such as warriors love. When Nanna, Balder's wife, saw the body wrapped in readiness for burning, her heart broke from her great grief, and the gods laid her, dead, beside her husband.

Then they lit the funeral fires with a thorn-twig, which is the emblem of sleep; and took their last look at the dead Balder as he lay upon the burning pyre. Odin, stepping forward, whispered in the unhearing ear of his son; but what he said no one ever knew.

When they tried to launch the ship, they found to their dismay that it was too heavily laden for their united efforts. So they sent for the mountain-giantess Hyrroken – who had ever been friendly to the people of Asgard – and begged her to grant this last service to the beloved of the gods. The giantess came, riding on a fierce wolf, with twisted snakes in her hands for reins. She gladly offered her help to the gods, and putting her shoulder to the prow, she gave it a mighty shove which sent the burning ship far out from the shore.

The flames rose higher and higher as the vessel drifted out toward the sea, bearing with it the light and joy of Asgard. A silence fell on all the watchers, and great sorrow filled their hearts.

All the world seemed under a shadow, and in the solemn stillness no sound was heard but the roaring of the flames on the burning ship. The gods stood upon the shore watching the funeral pyre, and, mingled with their sadness, was a dread foreboding of evil; for outside the ring of the shining ones of Asgard was another group of watchers – the frost-giants – who seemed to be looking on in mockery at the solemn rites, and now and then drew nearer, their tall forms looming up grim and threatening and terrible.

Then the sea and sky seemed to burst into one mass of glowing flame and a wonderful golden light spread over the earth as the fire upon the slowly moving ship burned each moment more brightly. Thus the vessel drifted westward toward the sea, and the gods knew that Balder had passed forever from their sight.

One by one they returned sadly to Asgard; but Odin could not give up his son without one last effort to reclaim him. He determined to go himself to Helheim, and offer a ransom to the goddess Hel if she would give Balder back to him. Meantime poor blind Höder had been mourning over the great evil which he had innocently wrought, and he wished with all the fervour of his loving heart that he could bring Balder back to Asgard. Sadly he sought the palace of his mother Frigga, and asked her whether he might not go to Helheim and offer his life to the dread goddess in exchange for Balder's. "The road is long and hard to find," said Frigga, "and what could a blind god do in the path where the best traveller would lose his way? Go back to your own dwelling, and send for Hermod, our swift messenger. He loved the shining Balder and now mourns for him. Bid him ride to Helheim."

Höder did as his mother commanded, and found Hermod only too willing to take the fearful journey for the sake of Balder. Odin gave him his own horse Sleipnir, who up to this time had never allowed another rider to mount him. Nine days and nights Hermod rode through the earth in darkness so thick that his horse could not see where to step. It was a black and steep and fearful road down to Helheim, and only on Odin's horse could the journey have been made. On the tenth morning he came to the golden bridge that spanned the river Giöll; and here a maiden, pale and sorrowful, kept guard. She halted Hermod as he rode across the bridge, and said:–

"Who are you, and what do you seek here among the dead? Yesterday five hands of men rode across the bridge, but they did not shake it as you alone have done. Your face is not as the face of the dead. Why do you come here? It is no place for the living."

Then Hermod asked if she had seen the shining Balder pass over her bridge; and the maiden answered –

"He has crossed it already, and has gone to the dark hall where the feast is now spread."

So Hermod rode on until he reached Hel's gloomy palace and came face to face with the terrible queen who ruled over the kingdom of the dead. Hermod trembled with fear as he looked about him, but his love for Balder gave him courage, and he stepped up boldly before the goddess, saying:–

"I have come to beg a boon of thee, O Hel. Your land is full without the shining Balder, and Asgard is empty and lonely since he has gone. Every heart mourns for him, and every eye is filled with tears. Give him back to us."

Slowly and sternly Hel replied: "Is there indeed no dry eye upon the earth? If it be true as thou sayest, that everything weeps for Balder, he shall return to Asgard; but if there is one who will not weep, he shall stay forever in Helheim."

Then Hermod hurried with the message back to Asgard, and when Odin heard the answer Hel had made, he gave the command, and everything upon the earth wept and mourned for Balder. Throughout the whole world arose the sound of bitter wailing; and not a single eye remained undimmed by tears. But among the mourners in Asgard there was one old woman whom Odin spied standing apart and shedding no tear.

"Weep," he cried, "weep for Balder that he may return."

"Nay," replied the old woman, "I will not weep. He has done naught for me that I should mourn him. Let him stay in Helheim." Then with a mocking laugh she hurried away, and Odin knew that it was Loki.

So Balder never came back to Asgard.

16

ANDVARI'S HOARD

Once Odin and Hoenir and Loki went on a visit to the earth, and in order to mingle freely with people without being recognized as gods, they laid aside all their divine powers and became, even in appearance, like ordinary men. When they had wandered about the earth many days, and talked with many people – who never knew, of course, that the gods were among them – they grew tired of the busy life of the world, and longed to find some place of quiet and rest. So they went far into the heart of the forest, and sat down beside a brook where many fish were leaping about and darting through the sparkling water. The gods lay idly upon the grass and watched them for a long time. Presently, they spied an otter sitting on the bank of the stream, lazily eating a fish which he had just caught. The gods looked on at the meal, and it made them remember that they too were hungry. Odin therefore proposed that they journey on in search of food, and to this the others readily consented; but as they rose to go, Loki suddenly took up

a large stone, and, throwing it at the otter, killed him instantly. At this wanton cruelty Odin became angry, and rebuked Loki for his act; but Loki only laughed, while he skinned the otter and cast its body back into the stream.

The gods then wandered on until almost nightfall before they came to any dwelling, and this was only a rude hut built on the side of a mountain. But they were too weary to look further, so they stopped to beg food and a lodging for the night. The old man who lived in the hut bade them enter and share his simple fare, and in return he asked them to tell him of their adventures. Without revealing their identity, Odin told him of their wanderings among men, and of the strange things they had seen. Hoenir also related many stories; but his were of brave heroes who had wrought the mightiest deeds on bloody battlefields. When it came Loki's turn, they asked him to tell all he knew of the life lived by the bright dwellers in Asgard, but Loki laughed and threw upon the ground his otter's skin. When the old man saw this, he cried out:–

"O wicked, cruel man, you have killed my son. He was fishing today in the stream, and at this sport he always takes the form of an otter. Alas, this is indeed he, and you have slain him."

Then he raised a loud cry, and called for help to his two sons, Fafnir and Regin, who came running in from the woods near by. As soon as they heard of the killing of their brother, they seized the three gods and bound them hand and foot, for, in becoming men, the gods had lost all their divine powers, and they had no choice but to yield.

When Odin begged the old man to ask whatever he would in payment for their ransom, both Fafnir and Regin demanded the life of one of the gods in return for their brother's. But their father spread the otter's skin upon the ground, and, turning to Odin, said –

"You and your wicked companions shall be free when you have covered every hair of this hide with a piece of gold or a precious stone."

"We will do this," answered Odin; "but first you must set one of us free that he may go and procure the treasure. Let the other two stay bound as hostages until he returns."

To this the old man and his sons agreed, and Odin bade them unbind Loki, for he alone would know where to find such vast treasure as they needed. Accordingly Loki was freed, and promising his companions to return with their ransom, he hurried away. There was only one place where a hoard of gold and precious stones might be found, and thither Loki directed his steps. There were many mountains to climb and rivers to cross before he reached the place he sought, and night coming on made the journey more difficult and wearisome.

At last he spied upon a rocky mountainside the thing he had come so far to find, a small, deep cavern in the rocks. As Loki drew nearer, the moonlight revealed a little brook gushing from the mouth of the cavern and winding in and out among the rocks below. It was small, but beautifully clear, and the pebbles in its bed shone in the moonlight like diamonds. Just where it issued from the cave, the water flowed swiftly over a deep pool, and here it was

so dark that only the sharp eyes of Loki could have caught the faint shimmer of a salmon which lay lurking in its depths.

Loki saw it, however, and his heart leaped for joy, for this salmon was no other than the cunning dwarf Andvari, the owner of a wonderful hoard of gold and gems. The treasure was buried somewhere near the cavern, and it was to gain this glittering hoard that Loki had come so far. So he now put forth all his skill to catch the wily salmon as it darted to and fro in the stream. The dwarf knew, however, who the fisherman was, and why he had come, and he had no intention of being caught and made to yield up his treasures. Loki spent many hours trying to lure the salmon into the shallows, but all his efforts were in vain. The crafty fish never moved from his deep, dark pool. Then Loki saw that further attempts would be useless unless he had help from some one with magic skill, so he determined to seek the aid of Queen Ran and her wonderful net.

Leaving the cave, he hurried down to the sea, and for many hours he walked along the shore, searching carefully among the rocks for the hiding place of the cruel ocean queen. Somewhere here, or upon the jagged reefs, he would be sure to find her spreading a net for her prey. But though he wandered for miles along the water's edge, he caught no glimpse of her anywhere; and, wearied and disheartened, he was about to give up his search, when he heard a low, rippling laugh just behind him, and turning he saw the beautiful daughters of the sea-king seated on the rocks combing their golden hair. Loki went over to them and begged them to tell him where he could find their mother, Queen Ran.

"Why do you seek her?" one of the maidens asked.

"Because I am a fisherman, and would like to ask her where the big fish are gathering now," replied Loki.

The sea-maidens laughed again and said:–

"O crafty, cunning Loki, do not think to deceive us who know well who you are, and why you have come hither. Play no tricks, then, and tell no lies to our mother, or you will not gain the object of your journey."

Loki promised, and begged the nymphs to tell him where to find Queen Ran, since no other than Odin himself needed her help.

"You must go about ten miles farther," answered one of the maidens, "until you come to a place where the rocks are high, and project in sharp, dangerous reefs far out into the sea. Here the waves dash with tremendous fury, and here is many a good ship wrecked and all her cargo lost. Look among the shadows of the rocks, and you will find our mother sitting there mending her net."

Loki thanked the nymphs and hurried on, for the night was growing black and the moon was completely hidden, and he had yet far to go. When he felt sure that ten miles lay between him and the daughters of the sea, he stopped and looked carefully about him. Near by was a group of tall, jagged rocks over which the waves dashed with great force; but there was one spot so protected that even the spray from the water did not reach it, and here Loki spied Queen Ran, long-fingered, greedy and cruel, mending her magic net. When she saw Loki, she tried to hide in the shadow of

the rocks, for she knew him and feared he had come with some unfriendly message from Odin. But Loki called to her and said:–

"Be not afraid, O Queen, for I come as a petitioner to beg a great boon of thee;" and Ran replied, "What does Loki wish, that he leaves the shining halls of Asgard to travel over the earth to speak to the wife of Aeger?"

"I have journeyed thus far," answered Loki, "because I have heard of your wonderful net. They say that it will catch whatever you wish, and that anything once caught cannot escape from its magic meshes. Therefore I have come to ask your help, for there is a certain salmon which I have long tried to snare, but which is too cunning to be caught by ordinary means. Lend me, I beg, your magic net."

"I cannot! I cannot!" cried Ran, "there is a ship sailing hither which will reach these rocks in the morning, and it is full of great treasure – jewels, and gold, and rich apparel. I have sent my mermaids to lure it to the reefs, where it will be dashed to pieces, and the prize be gathered into my net. No, I cannot lend it to you."

"But let me have it for just one hour," pleaded Loki, "and I will promise to return it in that time. I swear it on the word of a god."

The oath was reassuring, but still Ran hesitated to let the precious net leave her hands. At length, however, she was persuaded, and with many expressions of gratitude, Loki said good-by and hastened back to the cave of Andvari, for the night was now far spent, and at daylight the salmon would be sure to leave his haunts.

When he reached the cavern, the fish was still lying idly in the water, but upon seeing the net in Loki's hand it darted like a flash

down the stream. Then Loki quickly cast his net, and though the cunning fish swam with wonderful swiftness, it could not escape the magic net which began to close slowly and surely about it. As soon as Loki thought that his prize was secure, he drew the net on land, and, after slowly loosening the meshes, he at last grasped the struggling fish in his hand. Now, however, it was no longer a salmon fighting for its freedom, but the crafty dwarf Andvari. Anyone less wise than Loki would have dropped him immediately in surprise at the transformation, but Loki only held on the tighter, and shook the poor dwarf until he cried for mercy.

"No mercy will I grant thee, thou master thief," exclaimed the god, "until thou hast revealed to me the hiding place of thy ill-gotten treasures. Show me where it lies, or I will dash thee to pieces upon these rocks."

Seeing that there was no hope of escape, Andvari promised to yield up his hoard, and pointing to a large rock near by bade Loki raise it and look beneath. Without loosening his hold of the dwarf, Loki tried to lift the stone, but though it was far from being heavy or beyond his strength, he found that he could not move it. Then he knew that he was being tricked, and, grasping the dwarf still tighter, he shook him fiercely and commanded him to give his help. Andvari laid his finger on the stone and immediately it turned over and disclosed a large pit beneath.

It was quite dark now and the moon was completely hidden; yet even in the dim light Loki saw the sparkle of thousands of precious gems and the shimmer of many dazzling heaps of gold. It was truly a wonderful sight, and would have bewildered the

ordinary finder of such wealth; but Loki had no time to spend in admiration. He gathered all the treasure together in the net, which, by its magic power, grew larger and larger as he continued to fill it.

The dwarf, meanwhile, stood by sullen and angry, watching the gold and gems being poured into the net. Had it been Odin who was robbing him of his hoard, he would have begged that some small portion of it might be left him, but he knew better than to make such a request of Loki. So when the last of the treasure had been gathered up, he turned away and was disappearing into the woods when Loki caught the glitter of something upon his finger, and seizing him roughly, cried out: "Ho, ho, my cunning elf. So you would keep back some of the gems, I see. Yield me that ring upon your finger, or you shall not have one moment more to live."

Andvari's face grew black with rage, and he refused to give up his ring, stamping his foot all the while upon the ground and cursing Loki for his avarice and greed. Yet he knew too well that his fury was in vain, and soon he changed his tone, begging Loki, humbly, to leave him his one poor gem. This appeal would have moved any other of the gods, but Loki was never known to do a generous thing in all his life. He only gave a mocking, hateful laugh, and, seizing the dwarf, tore the ring from his finger.

It was a wonderful ring, shaped like a serpent, coiled, with its tail in its mouth. It had two blood-red rubies for eyes, and in the dim light they seemed to Loki to glow with all the cunning and cruelty of a living serpent. But this did not deter him from slipping the ring on his finger, and laughing triumphantly at the

dwarf, who was now foaming with helpless rage. Then Andvari cursed the ring and said:–

"May this ring be your bane, and the bane of all who shall possess it. May it bring sorrow and evil upon him who shall wear it, and from this day be the source of envy and hatred and bloodshed."

To these dreadful words Loki paid no heed, and, throwing his precious burden upon his shoulder, he hurried down the mountain side and sped swiftly on to the old man's cottage. Odin and Hoenir were still bound, and they had almost given up hope of Loki's return. But they forgot the tediousness of their captivity when they saw the great heap of gold and gems which Loki poured out of the net; for here was surely more than enough to cover ten otters' skins, and the remainder of the treasure would be their own.

Fafnir and Regin stretched the skin upon the ground, and bade Loki cover every hair. This seemed at first an easy thing to do; but the more gold and precious stones that Loki spread upon it, the larger the skin seemed to grow, until it covered the entire floor of the hut; and though Loki still added handfuls of gold, the brothers always found some spot uncovered. At last every hair of the hide was completely hidden beneath some coin or gem, and the gods demanded their release. The old man unloosed the cords which bound them and was bidding them depart, when Regin uttered a loud cry and declared that there was one hair yet uncovered upon the otter's head.

Odin and Hoenir looked at each other in dismay, for the net was now empty, and there was no way to procure further treasure.

Meanwhile, the old man and his sons were clamouring loudly for the gods to fulfil their promise. The case seemed indeed desperate; until Loki drew from his finger the serpent ring of Andvari, and laid it upon the hair. The brothers being now satisfied, the gods left the hut with all speed. Odin and Hoenir returned at once to Asgard, while Loki took back the net to Queen Ran, who was anxiously waiting, and reached her just as the dawn was breaking.

The treasure soon became, according to Andvari's words, a source of hatred and bloodshed; for the old man, wishing to keep the wealth for himself, drove his sons from the house, and shut himself up with his treasure. All day long he sat poring greedily over the heap of glittering gems, and running his fingers through the shining gold. Above all, he loved to watch the serpent ring, with its glowing ruby eyes.

Then one night Fafnir came suddenly upon him, demanding his share of the gold; and when the old man refused to yield up even one stone, Fafnir slew him in his anger, and took possession of all the treasure. Soon he grew fearful that his brother might steal upon him sometime and rob, or perchance kill him; so he changed himself into a monstrous dragon which breathed forth fire and spat deadly poison. Thus secured, he coiled himself about the hoard, and no one dared to approach him. Regin meanwhile fled to a neighbouring city, and became the king's master-smith, the maker of strong swords.

17

THE STORY OF SIEGMUND

The king whose protection Regin sought was named Alf, and when he learned of the great skill that belonged to this stranger in his realm, he gave Regin a place of honour among the sword-makers, and soon promoted him to be master-smith. Before many years passed the fame of Regin's smithy had spread far and wide; for here men gathered not only to learn the master's craft, but to share in that wisdom which he seemed to have gathered from all the ages. Even the noted wise men of the kingdom came to him, wondering at his great knowledge; and the king sought his counsel in all the difficult affairs of state.

At the court of King Alf lived his foster-son Siegfried, who was much beloved by the king, although he was not of his own blood. The youth was tall and strong, of fearless bearing, and with so keen an eye that men often quailed before his glance. His hair was golden red, and fell down in long locks over his shoulders; and his body was of a strength that matched the beauty of his face.

Men said of him that "never did he lose heart, and of naught was he afraid." When Siegfried grew to manhood, King Alf sent him to Regin's smithy that he might not only profit by the wisdom of this wisest of teachers, but also be taught to fashion a sword that could be worthily borne by one of his name and race, for Siegfried was the last of the Volsungs – a race of warriors whose fame was still fresh in the minds of men.

At first Siegfried did not like to wear the woollen coat and rough leather apron of a smith, for he was a prince's son and he thought the work menial; but he soon learned to respect his great teacher so much that the place took on a new dignity in his eyes and he no longer chafed at the hard work or the simple fare he shared with Regin. Early in the morning the sound of Siegfried's hammer could be heard as he worked blithely at his trade, and he almost forgot that he had ever known any other life than this one by Regin's side. When the long day was over and he sat with his master by the glowing light of the forge, Regin would tell him wonderful tales of gods and heroes and especially of the warrior race from which Siegfried sprang. Many times they sat until the last bit of fire in the forge sank into lifeless embers, and still the youth listened eagerly to the stories of brave deeds wrought by the long-dead Volsungs. The story which he never tired of hearing was that of his own birth, and in this way did Regin always begin the tale:–

There was once a mighty king named Volsung, who built a lordly palace such as men never saw before nor will ever see again; for its walls glistened with thousands of shields taken from his enemies in battle, and in the centre of the palace was a large courtyard in which grew a wonderful tree. This tree was so high that it towered above the castle walls, and its branches grew so thick that they spread like a roof over the whole palace. The king called this tree Branstock, and about its mighty trunk the Volsungs gathered to feast and sing songs in praise of their king and their race.

Ten sons and one daughter were born to King Volsung, and of these the great ruler was rightly proud, for the youths bid fair to excel their kinsmen in strength and courage, while the daughter, Signy, was so famed for her beauty that suitors came from many distant lands. Now there was a certain king named Siggeir, ruler of the Goths, who wooed the fair Signy with many rich gifts, all of which the maiden coldly disdained, for she distrusted his dark, evil-looking face. King Volsung, however, was much taken with the wealth of Siggeir and his seeming generosity, and he urged his daughter to accept this giver of rich gifts. For a long time Signy refused to listen to her father's words, but at length she yielded and was betrothed to her hated suitor. Then a great feast was proclaimed throughout the kingdom, and Siggeir gave freely of his gold. The wedding banquet was served in the courtyard beneath the spreading boughs of the mighty Branstock, and the guests were so many in number that they well-nigh filled the halls to overflowing.

When the feasting and merriment were at their highest, there suddenly appeared in the midst of the revellers a tall old man. He had a blue cloak thrown over his shoulders, and his beard was long and white. Only a few of the guests caught a glimpse

of his face, but those who did affirmed that he had only one eye. Stepping quickly up to King Volsung's wonderful tree, he drew from beneath his cloak a gleaming sword and drove it with great force into the tree trunk, up to the very hilt. Then turning to the astonished company, he said, "Whoso draweth this sword from the tree shall have it as a gift from me; and he shall find that he never bore in his hand a better sword than this." So saying, the old man went forth from the hall, and none knew who he was nor whither he went; but some whispered that it was Odin himself who had been among them.

Then one by one the guests of King Volsung tried to draw out the sword, but, though many of them were strong-armed warriors, not a single man had the power so much as to loosen it from the tree. King Siggeir was among the last to try his strength, and he strove until his eyes almost started from his head. But he, too, failed as the others had done, and returned to his place angered and humiliated at his defeat. When all the guests had been put to the test, and no one had drawn the sword, a certain lord said to King Volsung, "Have you no more sons?" and the king answered: "There is yet one more, but he is a mere lad. It would be cruel to shame him before so great a company." The warriors urged him, however, to summon the youth; and though anxious to spare his youngest son, the king reluctantly consented to have Siegmund appear. The lad stood straight and strong and fearless before the lordly company, and asked what was the king's will. Volsung pointed to the sword, and bade young Siegmund draw it forth. To the astonishment of all beholders, the lad stepped boldly up to the

Branstock, and, grasping the hilt of the sword, drew it out as easily as if it had only been in the scabbard. The guests were delighted at this evidence of Odin's favour toward an untried stripling; and they all praised Siegmund's good fortune – all but King Siggeir, who hated the youth from that day. He sought to buy the sword of Siegmund by offering him thrice its weight in gold, but the youth replied: "You might have had the sword if it were Odin's will that you should bear it. But now it shall stay mine, though you offered me all the gold you have." Then was King Siggeir filled with wrath at these scornful words and vowed vengeance against Siegmund and all the Volsungs.

When the wedding feast was over and the time came for Signy to set sail with her husband to his own land, King Siggeir spoke fair words to Volsung and his ten sons, and begged them to visit him in Gothland. Then said Signy to her father, "I pray thee, urge me not to go away with King Siggeir, for by my foreknowledge I am certain that no good will come of this marriage." But Volsung answered: "Speak not so, my daughter; and go with thy husband, for it will bring great shame to us if we fail to trust him without reason. Moreover, he will pay us back most evilly if we break faith with him for no cause." So Signy went with her husband, and they sailed away from the land of the Volsungs.

Now at the appointed time when the king had promised Siggeir to visit him in Gothland, Volsung and his ten sons put forth in the ships with a goodly following of men. After many days of pleasant voyaging, they reached the stranger's country, and came in toward the shore on the evening tide. But before they made a

landing, Signy the queen came secretly to them, and begged them to return at once to their own land, for Siggeir had sworn to kill them. Her pleadings were in vain, however, for the grisly old king of the Volsungs had never yet turned his back to a foe, and he had no fear of Siggeir and his hosts. So Signy went back to the palace, and the old king with his followers waited for the dawn. At a fitting time they left the boats, and sought the way to King Siggeir's palace. They seemed a gayly dressed company that had come as guests to a marriage feast, but under their cloaks each man carried a sword – being mindful of Signy's warning.

No messenger came forth to welcome them, but as they neared the palace King Siggeir fell upon them with a great army, and neither bravery nor a good sword could withstand the assault of such numbers. The Volsungs fought hard, and with all the courage of their race, and many a Goth lay dead at the old king's feet and at the feet of his sons; but at last Volsung himself was struck down by a treacherous blow; and when his followers saw their leader dead, they lost heart for the fight. Then all of the goodly company that had come to Gothland with the king were slain by Siggeir's men, and soon none were left of all the Volsungs but the king's ten sons. These were sorely wounded, yet alive, so they were bound with chains and carried before Siggeir that he might determine by what torment they should die.

Now came Signy to the palace hall and begged their lives of the king; but Siggeir laughed at her prayers and bade his men slay the sons of Volsung before their sister's eyes. But first he took from Siegmund the coveted gift of Odin, declaring that the youth should die by a stroke from his own sword. Then Signy threw herself at the feet of her lord and begged him to grant her brothers a few more days of life. At the end of that time he might do with them as he wished, and she would plead no more. To prove that she had no thought of trying to release them, she asked that they might be chained to a certain fallen oak in the forest so that she could visit them without incurring the king's displeasure. As all of the Volsungs were wounded, and some of them suffering greatly, this idea of prolonging their torment pleased Siggeir's fancy; and he agreed to let the brothers live for a few days chained to the fallen oak; but meantime he shut Signy up in the palace under a strict watch.

Now it happened that at midnight a she-wolf came out of the heart of the forest; and, seizing upon one of the Volsungs, devoured him, and then went her way. When news of this dreadful disaster reached Signy, she begged Siggeir to put her brothers in prison; but the king only laughed again and left the Volsungs in the forest. Each night, at midnight, the she-wolf came out of the deep woods to eat one of the brothers; and this was repeated until all were devoured except Siegmund. Then Signy called to her a trusted servant, and putting a pot of honey in his hand, she bade him go into the forest and smear the face and hands of her brother with the sweet liquid. The servant did as the queen instructed him; so that night, when the she-wolf came out of the forest, she smelt the sweet odour, and instead of falling upon Siegmund to tear him to pieces, she began to lick the honey from his face and hands.

Some of the liquid had dripped over Siegmund's lips, and when the she-wolf thrust her greedy tongue into his mouth, he caught

it firmly between his teeth and bit with all his strength. In her frantic efforts to get loose from the torturing grip, the she-wolf set her feet against the fallen tree and strained so mightily that the chain which bound Siegmund snapped in two pieces and the youth found himself free. Then he seized the wolf by the throat, and strangled her with his mere hands. Leaving the beast's body and his own torn clothes by the oak tree, he fled far into the forest.

King Siggeir believed that the last of the Volsungs had died in the same manner as his brothers; but Signy felt in her heart that Siegmund had succeeded, through her strategy, in escaping. Soon word was brought to her by her faithful servant that Siegmund was alive and in need of help; so each day she sent the messenger to the forest with food for her brother and the assurance that she would always watch over his needs. Then Siegmund built himself an underground hut in the woods, and lived as a wild man; and thither came Signy by night, for King Siggeir had granted the queen her liberty, believing that all the Volsungs were dead. Between them they plotted many things to avenge the murder of their kinsmen; but as yet their plans seemed futile, for how could one youth prevail against a king's army?

18

THE VENGEANCE OF THE VOLSUNGS

So, many years went by, and two sons were born to Signy and King Siggeir, both of them so like their father that the queen saw no touch of the Volsung spirit in either one, and no courage on which she could rely to help her and Siegmund in their work of vengeance. When the eldest was ten years old, his mother sent him to the forest that he might be trained by Siegmund if there were aught in him worthy of the Volsung race. When the lad came to the earth-dwelling, Siegmund saw that he had none of the right mettle in him; but he welcomed his sister's son and bade him make ready the bread for the evening meal while he himself went to seek firewood. On Siegmund's return the lad was still standing with the bag of meal in his hand, and there was no bread laid upon the coals. When Siegmund questioned him, he answered, "I dared not set hand in the sack, for there was something moving in the meal." So Siegmund sent the lad back to his mother, for

he knew that such a faint-hearted youth could never help him to avenge his murdered kinsmen.

Next year Signy sent her second son into the forest; but he too was fearful of the meal, and said on Siegmund's return, "There is something alive in the sack, so I dared not touch it." Then Siegmund bade him return to his mother. Some years later another son was born to Signy who in all ways resembled the Volsungs, so tall and strong and fierce he was, yet fair of face like Siegmund. When his mother deemed him courageous enough and of hardihood enough to stand an extreme test, she sewed his shirt to his skin and then suddenly tore it off, at which the child only laughed and said, "How little would a Volsung care for such a smart as that!" Then Signy knew that she might send the lad at once to her brother; so she bade him go forthwith to the earth house in the forest.

As soon as the lad, who was called Sinfiotli, came to Siegmund's hut, he was told to knead the meal for the baking, just as his brothers had been. Then he was left alone, and when Siegmund returned from gathering firewood, the bread was ready baked and lying on the hearth. When asked if he had seen anything move in the meal, the lad replied, "Yes, I felt there was something alive in the sack, but whatever it was I have kneaded it all together with the meal."

Then Siegmund laughed and said:–

"Naught wilt thou eat of bread this night, for thou hast kneaded up the most deadly of serpents. Though I may eat of any poison and live, there is no venom which thou mayst take and remain alive."

Now Sinfiotli stayed with Siegmund in the earth-dwelling, and was trained in all things that befitted a warrior of the Volsungs. Together they roamed the wild woods, hunting, fighting wild beasts and plundering like outlaws – for in no other way could they gain wealth. Sinfiotli soon forgot the days he had spent in King Siggeir's palace and believed himself in very truth a Volsung. Now it happened that one day as they journeyed together through the forest, they came upon a certain house in which lay two men fast asleep. On the wrists and ankles of the sleepers were heavy gold rings, and over their heads hung two grey wolfskins. By this Siegmund knew that they were werewolves and that this must be the tenth night – at which time the spell is removed and the enchanted may resume their human shape.

Then Siegmund and Sinfiotli put on the wolfskins while the men lay asleep; and having once done this, they could in no way free themselves from the enchantment until the appointed time. So they rushed forth into the forest howling like wolves, though each knew the meaning of the other's cries. Having the nature of wild beasts, they went in search of prey, but before taking their separate ways, they agreed to come to each other's aid in this way: that if more than seven men set upon either of the twain, he should howl in wolfish fashion so loud that his companion would hear him. So each went his way, and in time Siegmund met with a band of men who set upon him with spears; but he gave forth a deep, far-sounding howl that brought his fellow-wolf at once to aid him. Still in his wolfish shape, Sinfiotli killed everyone of the men who had attacked Siegmund, and once more the friends parted. Before he had gone far into the woods again, Sinfiotli was

suddenly surprised by eleven men with stout hunting gear; but so fiercely did he fight that in a short time the whole number were lying dead upon the ground.

As Sinfiotli, weary from the battle, lay under an oak tree, Siegmund came to him, and seeing all the dead men, straightway asked, "Why did you not howl to me for help?" And Sinfiotli answered, "I was loath to call on you for the killing of only eleven men." Then a sudden wolfish anger came over Siegmund, and he sprang upon Sinfiotli and bit him in the throat. But as soon as he saw his friend lying dead, he sorrowed greatly, and strove to bear the body on his back to the earth-house. The following day, as he lay at the door of the dwelling, he saw two weasels fighting, and one of them bit the other so that he died. Then the destroyer ran into a thicket and returned with a leaf in his mouth which he laid on the wound of the dead weasel. To Siegmund's surprise, it immediately sprang up well and whole. Then a raven flew overhead with a leaf of the same herb in his mouth, and this he dropped just at the werewolf's feet. So Siegmund took the leaf and laid it on Sinfiotli's wound, and he at once came to life again. Then the two waited until the day on which the enchantment was ended and they might cast off their wolf shapes. On this day they took the skins and burned them in the fire, that no further harm might come to any man through taking them.

Now by the time Sinfiotli had grown into manhood, Siegmund felt that the hour had come for avenging the death of the Volsungs, for he had tried the lad fully, and found no fear in him. So on a certain day they both left the earth-house and came late in the evening to King Siggeir's palace. They had no mind to walk at once into the king's presence, so they hid themselves among some casks of ale which were heaped up in the hall. While they lay thus hidden, Signy was aware of their coming; and as the king sat drinking deep she came out to them and spoke softly with them. Then they plotted together how they should slay King Siggeir, but the queen dared not stay long with them lest some servant should see her and tell it to the king.

Now that very night as the two children of Signy and the king were playing with a ball, one of the rings came off, and, rolling out into the hall, glided among the casks of ale. The children ran eagerly after it, but when they spied the two grim and well-armed men among the casks, they ran screaming to their father and told him what they had seen. Then the king grew fearful that some evil was awaiting him; and as he sat not knowing what to do, Signy led the children into the hall and said to her brother: "See, these two have betrayed you. Kill them, therefore." But Siegmund answered, "Never will I slay thy children for telling where I lay hid." Hardly had he spoken these words when Sinfiotli drew his sword and killed both the children. Then he took up the bodies and cast them at King Siggeir's feet. This sight roused such wrath in the king that he forgot his fear and ordered his men to seize hold upon the strangers and bind them with fetters.

So Siegmund and Sinfiotli were set upon by a great company of the king's men, but they fought so hard and bravely that many

bodies lay dead all around them, and those who were wounded long remembered this night's fighting. At last the strangers were overpowered and bound with strong chains. Then King Siggeir had them cast into a dungeon, while he pondered all through the night as to what form of death he could mete out to them. In the morning he had a great pit dug, and in the midst of it he stood on end a flat stone that reached from one side of the pit to the other, but was so high that none could climb over it. Then he set Siegmund in the pit on one side of the flat stone, and Sinfiotli on the other, and bade his men cover over the pit with turf, that they might be buried alive. But while the servants were laying on the turf, Signy came by with a bundle of straw in her arms. This she threw into the pit to Sinfiotli, and bade the servants say no word of it to the king. Then the covering of turf was laid on, and Signy went her way again.

As soon as he judged the night had come, Sinfiotli unwrapped the bundle of straw to make himself a bed; and as he groped through the bale in the darkness he found a great lump of swine's flesh. This he tore eagerly apart, for King Siggeir had given the captives naught to eat since they were taken prisoners. Then as he was rending the flesh in pieces, his fingers suddenly closed upon some hard steel; and when he drew it forth he found in his hand a sword. It was Siegmund's sword, the gift of Odin, which Signy had concealed in the straw unknown to the king. Sinfiotli uttered a cry of joy, and grasping the hilt firmly, he drove the point of the sword into the great rock that divided him from Siegmund. So fierce a blow did he deal that the sword cut through the stone up to the hilt; and by means of the great rent which it made, the two captives were able to speak with each other.

Then Siegmund grasped the blade of the sword, and together he and Sinfiotli worked all night until they had cut the great stone in half. When dawn came, they had sawed so fiercely that the sword-blade glowed in the darkness of the pit; and yet the keenness of its edge had never dulled. Soon Siegmund had cut a way through the turf and stones that covered the pit; and he and Sinfiotli stood together in front of King Siggeir's palace. There was no sound within, for all were yet asleep; so Siegmund and Sinfiotli crept softly into the hall carrying wood in their arms; and this they placed in great piles around the sleepers. Then they kindled a fire which spread quickly through the dry leaves and wood; and the smell of it awoke the sleeping men, who looked about and wondered why so thick a smoke was filling the hall. Soon the king was wakened by the loud screams of the women, and when he saw the smoke and flame he cried out:–

"Who has kindled this fire in which I burn?"

And Siegmund answered him from without the hall, "It is I, Siegmund the Volsung, with Sinfiotli, my sister's son; and now thou mayst know at last that all of my race are not dead."

Then he closed and barred the palace doors that none might escape, but first he begged Signy to come quickly out of the hall lest she should perish in the flames. And when she did not come, he offered her rich gifts and a place of honour among her own people; but Signy stood by the king's side and answered:–

"I have kept well in memory the slaying of the Volsungs, and

that it was King Siggeir who wrought the shameful deed. I sent two of my sons into the forest to learn how to avenge the wrong, and then came unto thee Sinfiotli who is a Volsung and none of King Siggeir's race. I also bade thee kill my young children, since their words had betrayed thee. For this and naught else have I wrought all these years that Siggeir might get his bane at last. Now vengeance has fallen upon him, but let the end come also to me, for merrily will I die with King Siggeir, though I was not merry to wed with him."

So Signy perished in the fire with her husband, and many died with them that the wrath of Siegmund the Volsung might be satisfied. Then he gathered together a great company of folk, and filled many ships with the treasures of King Siggeir, and with Sinfiotli he set sail for his own land. When he reached the country of the Volsungs, he found that a neighbouring king had usurped the throne, and was reigning in the old king's stead. Siegmund drove him from the country and himself took the throne of his father, where he ruled thereafter for many years. He and Sinfiotli waged war with other kings, and their fame spread abroad throughout the land. None could equal them in strength and valour, and of all the Volsungs King Siegmund bade fair to be greatest in renown.

* * * * *

As Regin spoke these last words, he turned to the youth at his side and smiled when he saw the glow of pride that shone in Siegfried's face as the master spoke of the brave deeds of the Volsungs.

"Shall I tell you the rest of the tale, and of how the sword of Odin failed your father in his need?" he asked, knowing well the answer Siegfried would make. Then the youth laid new coals on the fire; and the master resumed the oft-told tale.

19

THE MAGIC SWORD

So Siegmund became a mighty king – said Regin – and was known far and wide as the giver of rich gifts. In time of war he fought with Sinfiotli at his side; and when peace reigned in the kingdom, the son of Signy sat in the seat of honour by the king's throne. Now Sinfiotli loved a fair woman who was also wooed by the brother of Borghild, Siegmund's queen; and when they fought this matter out between them, Sinfiotli killed the queen's brother and took the maiden for his wife. Then Borghild demanded that the slayer be driven out of the kingdom because of this deed; but Siegmund said that the man was killed in fair fight, and therefore Sinfiotli should not pay the forfeit of banishment. Hoping to soften the queen's anger, he offered her gold and treasure as payment for her brother's life, but she would have none of it. Seeing, however, that she could not win her way with the king, she pretended to forgive the deed; and asked both Siegmund and Sinfiotli to the funeral feast which she held in her brother's honour.

There were many guests gathered to the feast, and Borghild, the queen, brought drink to each one. When she came to Sinfiotli with the great horn in her hand, she said, "Drink now, fair stepson." But when the youth looked into the horn he answered, "Nay, I will not, for the drink is charmed." Then the queen laughed and handed the horn to Siegmund, who drank the ale to the last drop, for no poison nor charmed drink could work him any harm. A second time did Borghild come to Sinfiotli with the horn in her hand offering him drink, and again he refused it, saying, "Guile is in the drink." So Siegmund took the horn and emptied it while the queen taunted Sinfiotli with his fears and said, "Why must other men drink thine ale for thee?" A third time Borghild came with the horn, and she goaded Sinfiotli with these words, "Drink now, if there is in thee the heart of a Volsung." So he took the horn, but when he looked into it, he said, "Venom is therein."

Now by this time Siegmund was so dazed with drinking that he had forgotten the queen's former hatred for her brother's slayer, and he cried to Sinfiotli, "Drink and fear naught." So Sinfiotli drank, and straightway fell down dead. When Siegmund saw the youth lying dead at his feet, his senses returned to him, and he sorrowed greatly over the words he had spoken. Then he lifted the body of Sinfiotli in his arms and bore it out of the palace hall while the funeral guests sat silent, none daring to intrude upon the king's sorrow. Now Siegmund fared on through the woods till he came to the seashore, and here he found a little boat with an old man seated at the oars. The man wore a dark blue cloak, and his hat was drawn down over his face; but Siegmund saw

none of this, for his thoughts were with his dead companion. The old man asked if they would be ferried to the other side of the bay, and Siegmund came with his burden to the water's edge. The little boat could not hold them all, so Siegmund laid the body of Sinfiotli beside the ferryman. But as soon as it was placed within, both the boat and the old man vanished, and Siegmund found himself alone. Yet his heart was full of gladness, for he knew that it was Odin himself who had come to take another Volsung to join the heroes in Valhalla. Then Siegmund returned to his own hall, and so hateful did the queen become in his eyes that he could bear the sight of her no longer and drove her forth from the palace. Not many months after this, word was brought to him that Borghild was dead.

Now there lived in a neighbouring country a wealthy king who had a daughter named Hiordis – the fairest and wisest among women. When Siegmund heard of the maiden's beauty, he desired to wed her, though he himself was now well on in years. So he chose the bravest warriors of his court, and with his horses well-loaded with gifts, he set out for the country where Hiordis lived. At her father's palace he was royally welcomed, and his proposals were received with favour; but there was another king suing for the maiden's hand, so no promise could be given to Siegmund. The father of Hiordis feared that, whichever of the suitors was rejected, war and trouble would arise, and therefore he knew not how to answer them. So he went to his daughter and said: "You are a wise woman, and I will let this matter rest in your hands. Choose a husband for yourself, and I will abide by your choice

though my whole kingdom be plunged into warfare." Then Hiordis answered, "Though King Lyngi is far younger than Siegmund, yet I will choose Siegmund for my husband, for his fame as a warrior is greater and we can rely upon his strength." So Hiordis was wedded to Siegmund the Volsung, and a great feast was held which lasted many days. King Lyngi departed to his own country, but Siegmund knew that he would hear of him again. After the wedding festivities were over, the Volsungs returned home; but they had been there only a few days before word was sent to Siegmund that King Lyngi had landed on his coast with a host of followers, and demanded that the Volsungs should meet him in battle.

Siegmund knew well that a great army had come against him, yet he answered that he would fight until no man was left in his kingdom; and accordingly he gathered his army together and met the forces of King Lyngi in an open field. The enemy rushed from their boats in such numbers that it seemed as if there was no end to them; and Siegmund saw that his followers would be no match for the great horde of fighting men that swept down from the enemy's ships. Nevertheless the Volsungs fought bravely when the horns blew that called the men to battle, and Siegmund, at the head of his army, cheered his followers on to the fight. He rushed boldly through the ranks of the foe, and no helmet or shield could withstand the stroke of his sword. So fiercely did he fight that none could tell the tale of those who fell before him, and his arms were red with blood even to the shoulders.

Now when the battle had raged a long while, there came a strange man suddenly into the midst of the fight. He had a blue cloak upon

his shoulders, and a slouched hat was pulled down over his face so that none might see he had only one eye. He advanced upon Siegmund with a shield held aloft; and the leader of the Volsungs – now sore spent with battle – knew not who the stranger might be, so he smote upon the upraised shield with all his strength. Never yet had the magic sword failed him in battle, but now it broke in half, and as its pieces fell to the ground, the stranger in the blue cloak disappeared. Then Siegmund knew who it was that had come against him, and he lost all heart for the fight. His men fell fast all around him, and although he fought on bravely, as became a Volsung, he saw that the battle was already lost. Soon he himself received a mortal wound, and when his men saw their leader drop from the ranks, they had no longer any hope of victory, and died fighting half-heartedly beside the fallen Siegmund.

Now Hiordis had left the palace with her handmaid when the battle first began, and she lay hidden in the forest where none of King Lyngi's people might find her. She had brought with her from the palace as much gold and treasure as she and her bondwoman could carry, that the conquering host might not enjoy the whole of Siegmund's wealth. When most of the Volsungs had fallen in battle, and King Lyngi knew himself victor, he hurried to the palace to take possession of Siegmund's riches and also Siegmund's queen. But when he entered the palace, he found everything in confusion. The treasure chests had been emptied, and none of the frightened servants could tell him what had happened nor where the queen might be found. So King Lyngi contented himself with what riches he found, and

that night his followers made merry in the halls of the Volsung, drinking ale and boasting of the day's victory.

When Hiordis heard the noise of the midnight revels, she crept out of her hiding-place and sought for Siegmund among the countless dead. The battle-field was a gruesome place, and she groped blindly and fearfully among the wounded, hoping that it might be here and not among the dead that she would find her lord. At last she came upon Siegmund, and tried to staunch the blood that still flowed from his wounds; but he put her aside, saying, "I will not suffer myself to be healed, since Odin wills that I should never draw sword again." Then the queen wept softly and answered, "If thou diest, who will then avenge us?" And Siegmund said: "Fear not that the last of the Volsungs has stood to do mighty deeds, for a son will be born to thee and me who shall be greater than all those who have been before him. Cherish carefully the pieces of Odin's sword which lie here beside me, for of these shall a goodly sword be made, and our son shall bear it, and with it he shall work many a great work so that his name shall be honoured as long as the world endures. Go now, for I grow weary with my wounds and would fain follow my kinsmen. Soon I shall be with all the Volsungs who have gone before me."

So Hiordis the queen kept silent, but she stayed beside Siegmund until the dawning; and when she knew he was dead, she took up the pieces of the broken sword and carried them back with her into the forest. Then she said to her handmaid: "Let us now change raiment, and do thou henceforth be called by my name and say that thou art the king's daughter. Look over there to the

sea, where some ships are now sailing toward our shores. Neither to King Lyngi nor to the strangers that are approaching would I be known as Siegmund's queen." Then the women changed raiment, and stood watching the ships as they neared the land.

The newcomers were not of King Lyngi's following, but were Vikings who had put into that coast on account of the high seas; and when they made a landing they came up over the shore and looked with wonder at the battle-field and the great number of the dead. The leader of the Vikings was Alf, the son of Hjalprek, king of Denmark, and as he gazed across the battle-field he saw the two women watching him, so he sent his men to bring them to him. When Hiordis and her handmaid stood before Alf, he asked them why they were standing thus alone, and why so many men lay dead upon the field. Then Hiordis, remembering the lowly position she had assumed, kept silent, but the handmaid spoke to him as befitted a king's daughter, and told him of the fall of Siegmund and the death of the Volsungs at the hand of King Lyngi and his hosts.

When Alf learned that the woman to whom he was speaking was of the royal household, he asked if she knew where the Volsungs' treasure was hid; and the handmaid answered that she had the greater part of it with her in the forest. So she led him to the spot where the gold and silver lay; and such a wonder of wealth was there that the men thought they had never seen so many priceless things heaped together in one place. All this treasure the Vikings carried to their ships; and when they set sail it was with the wealth of Siegmund on board as well as Queen

Hiordis and her handmaid. They spent many days on the sea before they reached Denmark, and during that time Alf spoke frequently with Hiordis and her maiden, but often he sat by the handmaid's side, believing her to be the king's daughter.

When the Vikings at last reached their own country, they were met by the queen mother, who listened gladly to the tale of their wanderings and welcomed the strangers to the palace. Before they had been home many days, she came to King Alf and asked him why the fairer of the two women had fewer rings and meaner attire than her companion. "For," she said, "I deem the one whom you have held of least account to be the nobler born." And Alf answered: "I, too, have doubted that she is really a bondmaid; for though she spoke but little when I first greeted her, she bore herself proudly like a king's daughter. But now let us make a trial of the two." So when the men were feasting that night, Alf left his companions and came and sat down by the women. Turning to the handmaiden, he said, "How do you know what is the hour for rising in winter when there are no lights in the heavens?" And the bondwoman answered, "In my youth I was wont to get up at dawn to begin my tasks, and now I waken as soon as the day breaks."

"Ill manners for a king's daughter," laughed Alf, and, turning to Hiordis, he asked her the same question.

The queen then unhesitatingly replied: "My father once gave me a little gold ring, and this always grows cold on my finger as the day dawns. Thus I know it is soon time to rise."

At these words King Alf sprang up, crying: "Gold rings are not given to bondmaids. Thou art the king's daughter."

Then Hiordis the queen, seeing that she could deceive Alf no longer, told him the truth concerning her history, and when he knew she was the wife of Siegmund he decreed that she should be held in great honour. Not long after this the son of Hiordis and Siegmund was born, and great rejoicing was made throughout the kingdom, for when the child was but a few days old, King Alf wedded Hiordis, whom he had found the worthiest of women. The boy was much beloved by his stepfather, and no one who looked upon him desired any other to succeed King Alf upon the throne, for the child was beautiful to see, brave and bold-looking, even as an infant. His eyes had already the keenness of a falcon, and so straight and strong he grew that the heart of King Alf was filled with joy.

When Regin reached this part of his story, he turned to Siegfried and laid his hand on the youth's shoulder, saying: "The gods have placed you among a kindly people, and given you a foster-father that has ever sought to train you in wisdom and in strength. But you are not of this people, and your place is not among them. Great deeds are in store for you, and you are to be worthy of your race. All that I could teach you, you have learned. Go forth, therefore, and by your own hand win fame that shall add to the glory of the Volsungs. Tomorrow you shall fashion a sword for your use, and it shall be mightier than any that has come from our hands. But let us drop the tale now and sleep, for it is almost daylight, and only a spark glimmers in the forge."

The next day Siegfried made ready the fire, but before he laid the steel in it he asked Regin what had become of the pieces of Odin's

famous sword. "No one knows where they are hidden," answered the master, "for on the death of your mother Hiordis, the secret was lost, and no man can tell where the place of their hiding may be." So Regin selected the very finest steel for Siegfried's sword, and the youth set to work eagerly, for Regin's story had filled him with a burning desire to go out into distant lands and do great deeds worthy of his name and race. For seven days and nights he never left his forge, but stood tempering and testing his steel, and throwing aside every piece that did not seem perfect. At last a blade was finished that promised to be worthy of a Volsung. Regin praised it highly and said he had never felt a finer edge. But Siegfried only said, "Let us prove it." So he took the sword and smote with all his strength upon the anvil.

The blade shivered into a dozen pieces.

Nothing disheartened, Siegfried set to work again, and spent many days and nights at his forge, often forgetting to eat or sleep in his eagerness to finish his task. When at last the steel had been finely tempered and seemed of perfect workmanship, he called to Regin and bade him try its strength. "Nay, let us not dull the edge," replied the master; "there is no need to put it to the test, for I can see that it is true and strong." But Siegfried took the sword and smote again upon the anvil; this time the blade was blunted, though it did not break in pieces. Then Regin besought him to try no longer, but the youth, grim and determined, returned to the forge and made ready his tools for another effort.

That night he paused many times in his work, and often felt so discouraged that he was tempted to give up the task; but each time he became ashamed of his weakness, and bravely set to work again. Once when he sat down by the fire to rest, he was conscious of some one's being in the room, but thinking it was Regin who had come to inspect his work, he did not look up to see. At length, however, the silence grew uncomfortable, and Siegfried turned around. Close beside him was standing a tall man wrapped in a dark blue mantle. His beard and hair were very long and very white, and by the dim light of the fire Siegfried noticed that he had only one eye. His face was kindly, and his whole presence had an air both gentle and reassuring, yet something about him filled the youth with a strange awe. He waited for the stranger to speak, but no word came, and Siegfried began to tremble with nervous fear. At this the old man smiled, and handed him the pieces of a broken sword. Siegfried took them in wonder, but before he could frame a question he found himself suddenly alone; the stranger had disappeared.

The next morning Siegfried hastened to Regin and told him of his strange visitor. Regin thought at first that the lad had been dreaming, but when he saw the pieces of broken sword, he cried out joyfully:–

"Fortune now be with you, Siegfried; for it was no other than Odin who visited you, and these pieces are of the famous sword which in former days the ruler of the gods gave to your father. There is no fear for your future now, since Odin has chosen to watch over your welfare; and by his decree you will stand or fall."

Grasping the pieces of Odin's sword firmly in his hand, Siegfried welded them together into a mighty weapon, the strongest that

had ever come from the hand of man. And he called the sword Balmung. Then he bade Regin test the mettle of the new blade, and when the master looked upon it, it seemed as though a fire burned along the edges of the sword. Now Siegfried grasped the weapon in his two hands and smote with all his strength upon the anvil, but no pieces of steel fell shattered at his feet, for the sword had cut the anvil in two as easily as if it had been a feather. So Siegfried was satisfied.

20

THE SLAYING OF FAFNIR

One day Regin said to Siegfried, "You have forged for yourself the famous sword Balmung as your father Siegmund foretold. Now it remains for you to fulfil the rest of the prophecy and win fame that will add glory to the name of the Volsungs. Of my celebrated wisdom you have already learned all there is of worth, and there are no ties to hold you to this people; but before you leave the land which has nourished you, there is one more task which I would fain lay upon you – the slaying of the dragon which guards a wonderful treasure."

"How can I start out upon adventures with nothing but a sword, even though that sword be Odin's gift?" asked Siegfried. "I have no horse, and I should make a sorry appearance if I went on foot."

"Go out into yonder meadow," said Regin, "and there you will find the best steeds that King Alf has gathered either by purchase or as the spoil of battle. Choose yourself one from among them; they are all of noble race."

Siegfried went over to the meadow where the stately horses were grazing, and saw that each one of them was truly fine enough to be the charger of a king's son. Indeed, they all seemed to him so desirable that there was none which he would prefer above another. While he was hesitating, he heard a voice at his side ask, "Would you choose a steed, Sir Siegfried?"

Siegfried turned quickly around, for he had not heard anyone approaching, and his heart beat fast when he saw beside him a tall form wrapped in a blue mantle. He dared not look closer, and he trembled now with both fear and joy, for the form and voice were strangely familiar. Then falteringly he answered:–

"I would indeed choose, but all the horses seem to me to be of equal beauty and strength."

The stranger shook his head and said: "There is one horse here which far surpasses all the rest, for he came from Odin's pastures on the sunny slopes of Asgard. He it is you must choose."

"Gladly would I do so," replied Siegfried, "but I am too ignorant to know which he is."

"Drive all the horses into the river," said the old man, "and I think you will then find the choice easy."

So Siegfried drove them out of the meadow, and down a steep bank into the stream below. They all plunged in boldly, but soon began to struggle frantically against the current which was bearing them rapidly down the river upon a bank of rocks below. Some of the horses turned back when they felt the force of the water; some fought helplessly against it and were carried down toward the rocks; but one swam to the other side and sprang up on the green bank. Here he stopped a moment to graze, then he plunged again into the stream, and, breasting the current with apparent ease, he swam to the shore and stood at Siegfried's side.

The youth stroked the stately head and looked into the large, beautiful eyes. Then turning to the stranger he said, "This is he."

"Yes," replied the old man, "this is he, and a better steed did man never have. His name is Greyfel, and he is yours as a gift from Odin."

So saying, the strange visitor disappeared, and Siegfried returned to his forge full of joy and pride, for he knew that no other than the Father of the Gods himself had come to direct his choice.

When Regin heard of this second visit of Odin's he said to Siegfried:–

"You are truly blessed and favoured of the gods, and it may be that you are the one chosen to perform the task of which I have already spoken to you. I have cherished the hope for many years that in you I might find one brave enough to face the dragon, and restore the treasure to its rightful owner." Then he told Siegfried of Andvari's hoard, and of how it came to be guarded by the dragon Fafnir. "This monster," he continued, "does not rest satisfied with the possession of his treasure, but must needs live upon the flesh of men; and he has thus become the terror of all the country round. Many brave men have sought to slay him for the sake of the gold, but they have only miserably perished; for the dragon breathes out fire which will consume ten men at a breath; and he spits forth poison so deadly that one drop of it can kill. He is, as I have told you, my brother, but nevertheless I bid you slay him."

"I will go," cried Siegfried, eagerly; "for though the monster be all that you have said, with Greyfel and my sword Balmung I fear neither man nor beast."

The following day Siegfried bade farewell to King Alf and started on his journey, taking Regin with him, since the latter knew the road so well and could guide him to the dragon's cave. They travelled for many days and nights, and at last came to a narrow river whose current was so fierce that no boat, Regin said, was ever known to brave its waters. But neither Siegfried nor Greyfel felt a touch of fear, and the noble horse carried both riders safely to the opposite bank. Here they found themselves at the foot of a tall mountain, which seemed to rise straight up like a wall from the river's edge. It was apparently of solid rock, for no tree or shrub or blade of grass grew upon its steep side. There were no sounds of birds in the air, no sign of any living thing inhabiting this dreary place; nothing to see but the rushing river over which the mountain cast its gloomy shadow. It was enough to dishearten the stoutest hero, but Siegfried refused to turn back, though Regin, now trembling and fearful, besought him to give up the adventure.

They went on some distance farther along the river bank, to a place where the mountain appeared less rocky and forbidding. There were patches of earth to be seen here and there, and occasionally a straggling tree sought to strike its roots into the unfriendly soil. Pointing up through the trees, Regin said:–

"Look close and you will see what seems to be a path worn in the earth. It reaches from the mountain top down to the water's edge, and it is the trail of the dragon. Over this he will come tomorrow at sunrise, but think not to encounter him face to face, for you could not do it and live. You must depend upon stratagem if you would hope to slay him. Dig, therefore, a series of pits and cover them with boughs, so that the dragon, as he rushes down the mountain side, may fall into one of them and not get out until you have slain him. As for me, I will go some distance below, where the view of Fafnir's cave is plainer, and I can warn you of his approach." So saying, he went away, and Siegfried remained alone, wondering at Regin's cowardice, but content to face the danger with only the help of Balmung.

It was now night, and the place became full of unknown terrors. Even the stars and the moon were hidden by thick clouds, and Siegfried could hardly see to dig his pits. Every time he struck the earth, the blow brought a deep echo from the mountain, and now and then he heard the dismal hoot of an owl. There was no other sound save the noise of the swiftly running river, and his own heavy breathing as he worked away at his task.

Suddenly he was aware that some one was standing beside him, and when he turned to look, his heart beat fast with joy, for even in the darkness he fancied he saw the blueness of the stranger's coat, and his long, white beard beneath the hood.

"What are you doing in this dismal country, Sir Siegfried?" asked the old man.

"I have come to slay Fafnir," replied the youth.

"Have you no fear, then?" continued the stranger, "or no love for your life that you risk it thus boldly? Many a brave man has

met death ere this in the perilous encounter you would try. You are young yet, and life is full of pleasures. Give up this adventure, then, and return to your father's hall."

"No, I cannot," answered Siegfried. "I am young, it is true, but I have no fear of the dragon, since Odin's sword is in my hands."

"It is well said," replied the old man; "but if you are to accomplish the slaying of Fafnir, do not dig any pits here on the river's bank, for it will be of no avail. But go up on the mountain side until you have found a narrow path worn deep into the earth. It is Fafnir's trail, and over it he is sure to come. Dig there a deep pit, and hide in it yourself, first covering the top with a few boughs. As the dragon's huge body passes over this, you can strike him from beneath with your sword."

As the stranger finished speaking, Siegfried turned to thank him, but he saw no one there; only Greyfel was standing at his side. But his courage now rose high, for he knew that it was Odin who had talked with him. He hurried up the mountain side and soon found the dragon's trail. Here he dug a deep pit and crept into it himself, covering the top as Odin had directed. For hours he lay still and waited, and it seemed to him that the night would never end. At last a faint streak of light appeared in the east, and it soon grew bright enough for Siegfried to see plainly about him. He raised one corner of his roof of boughs and peeped cautiously out. Just then there came a terrible roar which seemed to shake the whole mountain. This was followed in a moment by a loud rushing sound like some mighty wind, and the air was full of heat and smoke as from a furnace. Siegfried

dropped quickly back into his hiding-place, for he knew that the dragon had left his cave.

Louder and louder grew the fearful sound, as the monster rushed swiftly down the mountain side, leaving smoke and fire in his trail. His claws struck deep into the ground, and in his rapid descent he sometimes tore up the roots of trees. His huge wings flapping at his side made a frightful noise, while the black scaly tail left behind it a track of deadly slime. On he went until, all unknowing, he glided over the loosely strewn boughs which covered the pit, and Siegfried struck with his good sword Balmung. It seemed to him that he had struck blindly. Yet in a moment he knew that the blow was sure and had pierced the monster's heart, for he heard it give one roar of mortal pain. Then, as he drew out his sword, the huge body quivered an instant and rolled with a crash down the mountain side. But in drawing out his sword from the dragon's heart, a great gush of blood followed which bathed Siegfried from head to foot in its crimson stream. He did not heed this, however, but sprang out of the pit and hurried down to where the dragon, so lately a thing of dread and horror, now lay apparently lifeless at the foot of the mountain.

When Fafnir was aware that he had received his death-wound, he began to lash out fiercely with his head and tail, in hopes that he would thereby kill the thing which had destroyed him. But Siegfried stayed at a safe distance; and when he saw the dragon cease its frantic struggles and lie quiet on the ground, he came nearer and gazed at it in wonder and half in fear – for Fafnir, though dying, was still a terrible creature to look upon.

The dragon slowly raised its head as Siegfried approached, and said, "Who art thou, and who is thy father and thy kin that thou wert so bold as to come against me?" At first Siegfried was loath to tell his name; but soon he felt ashamed of his fears and answered boldly:–

"Siegfried I am called, and my father was Siegmund the Volsung." Then said Fafnir, "Who urged thee to this deed?" and Siegfried answered, "A bold heart urged me; and my strong hand and good sword aided me to do the deed."

Now Fafnir knew well who it was that had set the youth upon this adventure, and he said: "Of what use is it to lie? Regin, my brother, hath sent thee to work my death, for he is eager to gain the treasure which I guarded these many years. Go, therefore, and seek it out, but first I will give thee this counsel; turn away thy steps from this ill-fated gold, for a curse rests upon it, and it shall be the bane of everyone that possesses it." As he spoke these words, Fafnir gave a fearful shudder that seemed to make the trees around him tremble; and in a moment Siegfried saw that the great dragon was dead.

Then Regin crept out of his hiding-place, and drew near to the dead creature, peering closely into the dull, glazed eyes to see if it were really a thing no longer to be feared. A look of hatred came into his face, but it disappeared quickly when he turned to the youth at his side and said:–

"Bravely done, Siegfried! You have this day wrought a great deed which shall be told and sung as long as the world stands fast." Then he added eagerly, "Have you found the hoard?"

"I did not look for it," answered Siegfried; "for after what I have been told of the curse which rests upon it, I had no desire to touch it."

Regin seemed now to be trembling with excitement, and he exclaimed hurriedly: "We must seek it at once, yes, at once, before anyone can come to claim it and we thereby lose a wonderful treasure. But let me go alone to find it, for you would surely lose your way." Then as he saw Siegfried wiping his blood-stained sword on the earth, he grasped the youth's arm fiercely and said: "Do not put the blade into its sheath until you have done one thing further. While I am searching for the cave, do you cut out Fafnir's heart and roast it, that I may eat it upon my return."

While he was speaking, Regin's face had lost its usual gentle and kindly look, and had become crafty and sly and full of cruel cunning. He now looked suspiciously at Siegfried, but the youth turned his head away, for he could not bear to look on at such a dreadful transformation. Meanwhile Regin was muttering to himself: "The gold! the gold! and precious gems in great glittering heaps! All of Andvari's hoard is mine now – all mine." And he hurried away, leaving Siegfried surprised and sorrowing to find how soon the curse of that ill-fated gold had fallen on its would-be possessor.

When Regin had gone, Siegfried set to work to roast Fafnir's heart, and when the dreadful meal was cooked, he laid it upon the grass, but in so doing, some of the blood dropped upon his hand. Wondering what taste there could be in the dragon's heart to make Regin desire to eat it, Siegfried put the finger, on which

the blood had dropped, to his lips. All at once he heard a hum of voices in the air. It was only a flock of crows flying overhead and chattering to themselves, but it sounded like human voices, and Siegfried could plainly tell what the crows were saying. A moment later two ravens came flying by, and he heard one of them say, "There sits Siegfried roasting Fafnir's heart that he may give it to Regin, who will taste the blood, and so be able to understand the language of birds."

"Yes," replied the other raven, "and he is waiting for Regin to return, not knowing that when Regin has taken possession of the hoard, he will come back and slay Siegfried."

The youth listened to these words in sorrow and surprise, for in spite of the look which he had seen on Regin's face, he could not believe his master guilty of such murderous thoughts.

Soon Regin returned, but what a change had come over him. Siegfried saw that the raven's words were indeed true, and that the curse of Andvari had fallen upon the new possessor of the hoard. If Regin's face had been mean and crafty before, it was now ten times more dreadful, and his mouth wore an evil smile which made Siegfried shudder. It seemed, too, as if his body had shrunk, and its motion was not unlike the gliding of a serpent. He was talking to himself as he came along, and appeared to be counting busily on his fingers. When Siegfried spoke, he looked up and eyed him furtively, then his face became suddenly black with rage, and he sprang at the youth, crying:–

"Fool and murderer, you shall have none of the gold. It is mine, all mine."

With the strength of a madman he dashed Siegfried upon the ground, and seizing a large stick struck him with all his force. But Siegfried sprang up quickly and, drawing Balmung, prepared to defend himself against Regin's attack. Enraged now to the point of frenzy, Regin struck again and again, and suddenly, in his blind fury, rushed upon Siegfried's sword. Siegfried uttered a cry of horror and closed his eyes, for he could not look upon the painful sight. When he opened them again, Regin was lying dead at his feet. Then he drew out his sword, and, sitting down beside his slain friend, wept bitterly. At length he arose, and mounting Greyfel rode sorrowfully away.

The good horse bore him straight to Glistenheath – to the cave where Fafnir had hidden the ill-fated hoard. Here he found gold and gems in such heaps that his eyes were dazzled, and he turned away fearing to burden himself with the treasure and the curse which rested upon it. But from the pile he took Andvari's ring, which he placed upon his finger, and a gold helmet. He also chose from the treasures of the hoard a magic cape and a shield. Then he remounted Greyfel, after placing upon him as many sacks of gold as the horse could well carry.

21

THE VALKYRIE

For many days Siegfried travelled on, saddened and discouraged, and having no heart for further adventures, since his first one had ended so sadly. He felt that he cared but little what became of him, and, letting the reins lie loose on Greyfel's neck, he allowed the horse to carry him wherever it would. At night he rested under the shade of the forest trees, and by day he wandered aimlessly over the country, too disheartened even to wish to return to King Alf's court again. But although he did not care to guide Greyfel, the horse was being led by a hand far wiser than his own, for Odin had other tasks in store for Siegfried, and it was he who now directed the young hero's path.

One day at nightfall they came to the foot of a mountain and Greyfel stopped, as if waiting for his master to dismount. Siegfried, not wishing to rest here, urged his horse forward; but, for the first time, Greyfel refused to obey. His master, wondering at this stubbornness, but too tired and indifferent to force him

further, dismounted and prepared to remain where he was for the night. Something about the place, its loneliness and silence, recalled the other mountain side where his first deed of glory and his first great sorrow had come to him. He could not sleep, so he wandered about among the trees, now and then stopping to listen as some sound broke the stillness of the night.

Once when he was looking toward the mountain top, he fancied he caught the glimmer of a light somewhere among the trees; and as he watched it longer, he saw what appeared to be tongues of flame leaping up and then disappearing. Alert now, and eager to get nearer this strange sight, he mounted Greyfel and directed him toward the fire. The horse obeyed readily, seeming to know the way; and when Siegfried drew nearer, he found that this was no common fire, but a circle of flames enclosing a large rock. There was no path up the mountain, and Siegfried felt uncertain whether to proceed. The horse, however, did not hesitate, but began the ascent boldly, picking his way among the trees and over the fallen trunks; sometimes stumbling and sometimes bruising his legs, but never once faltering or showing a desire to turn back.

Suddenly Siegfried felt upon his face a scorching wind followed by thick smoke that blinded his eyes. A quick turn of Greyfel's had brought them almost upon a wall of leaping flames, which rose so high that Siegfried could see nothing beyond them. The intense heat burned his face, and he dared not open his eyes to look about him. Greyfel snorted and pawed the ground, then suddenly made a movement forward as if to plunge into the flames. For an instant Siegfried thought of the prophecy made by his father Siegmund

that he should be the greatest of the Volsungs, and he hesitated to risk his life thus lightly. Then he felt ashamed of the momentary cowardice, and with but one quick throb of fear at the peril he was rushing into, he bent forward and spurred Greyfel into the fire.

It was all over in an instant. He felt the scorching flames lick his face, and then he heard the horse's feet strike upon solid rock. When he opened his eyes to look about him, he realized that he had ridden through the fire all unharmed, and he was full of wonder at his safety. Greyfel, too, was unhurt; not a single hair upon his mane was singed; and Siegfried offered a silent prayer to Odin, who had guided them through such peril.

He dismounted and looked about, and found that he was standing upon the rock which he had seen from below, and which he now discovered to be completely encircled by the wall of fire. But stranger even than this was the sight of a man lying full length upon the rock, and seemingly unconscious of the fire which was raging all around him. His shield was on the ground beside him, but his helmet covered his face so that Siegfried could not tell whether he was dead or sleeping. His figure was youthful and his dress of richest texture, while the armour which he bore seemed too fine to bear the brunt of warfare.

For a long time Siegfried stood beside the unconscious figure, wondering whether he had best awake the sleeper, or go away and leave him undisturbed. At last his curiosity became too strong, and, lifting the youth gently, he raised the helmet and gazed with wonder and delight at the beautiful face beneath. Then, as the sleeper did not awake, Siegfried took off his helmet, hoping thus

to rouse him; but what was his surprise to see a shower of long golden hair fall down over the shoulders of the seeming youth. He started back so suddenly that the maiden awoke, and looking up at Siegfried said softly, "So you have come at last."

The young hero was too astonished to make any reply, but remained kneeling beside her, waiting for her to speak again. He wondered whether she was really human, or only some spirit of the night. Seeing his surprise, the maiden smiled, and, seating herself upon the rock, she pointed to a place beside her and said:–

"Sit down, Sir Siegfried, and I will tell you my story, and how I came to be sleeping in this strange place."

Still wondering, especially at hearing himself thus addressed, Siegfried obeyed, and the maiden began:–

"My name is Brunhilde, and I am one of Odin's Valkyries, or choosers of the slain. There are eight of us who do this service, and we ride to battle on swift-winged horses, wearing such armor as warriors carry, except that it is invulnerable. We go into the midst of the fight even when it is fiercest, and when any of the heroes whom Odin has chosen are slain, we raise him from the battle-field, lay him before us on the horse, and ride with him to Asgard, to the place called Valhalla. This is a beautiful hall made of gold and marble, and it has five and forty doors wide enough for eight hundred warriors to march in abreast. Inside, its roof is made of golden shields, and its walls are hung with spears of polished steel that give a wonderful bright light to all the hall. Every day the warriors drink of the mead which is prepared for the gods themselves, and they feast on the meat of a wonderful boar which

is daily slain and boiled in the great caldron, and which always comes to life again just before the heroes are ready to eat.

"Sometimes Odin sits at the board and shares the feast with them, and when the Valkyries are not doing service on the battle-field, they lay aside their armor and clothe themselves in pure white robes, to wait upon the heroes. When the feast is over, the warriors call for their weapons, and spear in hand they go out into the great courtyard, where they fight desperate battles and deal terrible wounds, performing deeds of valour such as they achieved while on the earth. Since in Asgard there is no dying, every combatant who receives some terrible wound is healed at once by magic power. Thus the heroes share the blessings and privileges of the gods, and live forever, having won great fame and glory.

"Now there was a certain battle being waged in a country far from here, in which the combatants were an old warrior named Helm Gunnar, and a youth called Agnar. Odin had commanded me to bear Helm Gunnar to Valhalla, and leave the other to the mercy of the conquerors. The youth of Agnar moved me, however, to pity; so I left the old warrior upon the battle-field, though he was already sore wounded. Then I lifted Agnar from the ground, and, laying him upon my horse, I carried him to Asgard.

"In punishment for my disobedience and daring, the All-Father took from me forever my privilege of being a Valkyrie, or shield-maiden. He also condemned me to the life of a mortal, and then he brought me to this rock, where he stung me with the sleep-thorn, and made this my sleeping place. But first he surrounded

the rock with a wall of fire, and he decreed that I should sleep here until a hero who knew no fear should ride through the flames and waken me. I am well versed in the lore of runes, and I read there long ago that he who knows no fear is Siegfried, the slayer of Fafnir. Therefore thou art Siegfried and my deliverer."

For a long time Brunhilde talked with him, and told him many wonderful things, of the noble deeds of heroes and of bloody battles fought in far-off lands. Then, knowing that he was but a youth in spite of his brave acts, she imparted to him something of the wisdom she had gained as "one of the greatest among great women" – for thus it was that men spoke of her. She warned Siegfried of the dangers he would encounter on his journey, and bade him beware of the wiles of those who would call themselves his friends. She charged him to abide always by his oath, "for great and grim is the reward for the breaking of plighted troth."

"Bear and forbear, and so win for thyself long, enduring praise of men.

"Give kind heed to dead men – sick-dead, sea-dead, or sword-dead."

Thus spoke Brunhilde, and Siegfried listened, and ever, as she stopped speaking, he begged to hear still more. Then she read for him many things written in the runes, and Siegfried listened, marvelling at her wisdom.

The circle of fire had now burnt itself out, but daylight had come, and Siegfried could plainly see the perilous ascent he had made up the mountain. Brunhilde took his hand and bade him farewell, but, before she left him, Siegfried put upon her finger

the ring which he had taken from Andvari's hoard. Then he watched her depart toward her castle in Isenland, feeling very lonely, and wishing he might follow her. But Greyfel's head was turned a different way, and Siegfried knew that Odin had other things for him to do, so he allowed the horse to carry him away from Brunhilde's country, though he would fain have gone thither. And Siegfried longed for the maiden, and sorrowed at parting from her; but Brunhilde, though she loved him well, bade him go his way, since thus it was written in the runes that not she, but another, should be the wife of Siegfried.

22

SIEGFRIED AT GUNTHER'S COURT

For several days Siegfried rode across the country without meeting anyone who could tell him in what land he was, or whither the roads would lead him. At times he longed to return to the palace of King Alf, and again he hoped that Odin was conducting him to new adventures which would prove that his father Siegmund had not prophesied great things of him in vain. He was growing very weary of the continued stretch of forest and mountain that never seemed to end, and he began to wonder whether his dream of greatness was not, after all, a thing of shadows – a mere will-o'-the-wisp, which it would be foolish for him to follow. Yet Odin's sword was in his hand, and the strange blue-cloaked old man had already come to help him when he was most in need of guidance. So, not knowing, himself, in which direction to go, he let the reins lie loosely on Greyfel's neck, and trusted to Odin to lead them.

Soon the forest ended and they came out into the open country where Siegfried hoped he might meet with some one who could

tell him whither he was faring. The landscape now changed to meadows and ploughed fields, with here and there a castle perched high on the protecting hills. Siegfried kept as much as he could on the well-travelled roads, since there he would be most likely to meet with some other rider who could direct his way; but all those whom he saw seemed to be wanderers, like himself, and they could tell him little of the country or the people. In return, they would ask him whither he was going, and what was the object of his journey, but to all questions he offered no reply save that he was travelling in search of adventures. But at heart he had no desire for adventures, unless they led him among people and into the life of the world. He had grown weary of his solitude and his aimless wandering, and longed for the companionship of men.

One day, late in the evening, he found himself on the edge of a thick forest. He did not wish to enter this, for it looked dark and impenetrable, and already Greyfel was picking his way among brambles and over uncertain ground; so he turned the horse's head and prepared to go back to the road he had lately left. But Greyfel knew better than his master where to go, and persisted in moving forward into what seemed to be the very heart of the forest. In a moment, however, Siegfried found that they were not stumbling helplessly about, for he heard the sharp, clear sound of the horse's hoofs upon a hard road, while the glimmer of many lights in the distance told him he was not in a forest wilderness, but near some great city. Soon he met a man on horseback, and inquired of him what country this was, and whither the road would lead him.

"This is Burgundy, sir," answered the stranger, "and yonder is the city where King Gunther himself dwells. There you are sure of finding shelter and entertainment for the night." Siegfried thanked him, and spurred Greyfel toward the city.

In the palace of King Gunther, a great feast was being held. There was wine in costly beakers, and meat served upon plates of gold. At the place of each guest was a silver goblet, and these were often lifted high as the company drank to the health of Gunther and all his noble race. While the men feasted and drank, the women of the household stood at the palace windows looking down the road to see if some strolling minstrel might not be passing by who could be summoned in to help them beguile the weary hours that would follow the days of feasting.

The king's mother, Queen Ute, was busy with her loom, for she cared no longer for the gayety of the palace nor for any entertainment that some wandering harper might provide. She was a wise woman, learned in magic arts and the reading of dreams.

One day when her daughter, Kriemhild, the beautiful sister of King Gunther, came to her with troubled face, she asked the maiden why she seemed so sad, and Kriemhild answered: "I dreamed last night that a hawk with feathers of gold lighted on my wrist; and naught was so dear to me as this hawk. And I dreamed that I told both you and the king, my brother, that I would cast aside all my rich raiment and gems rather than lose the hawk that was feathered with gold."

Then said Queen Ute, the witch-wife: "Trouble not yourself over strange dreams. A hero is coming to woo you, and he shall stay at your side even as the hawk upon your wrist."

Now on this day when King Gunther was feasting, and the women idly watched the long white line of road where often a gallant horse and rider came galloping toward the castle gates, the fair Kriemhild suddenly exclaimed that some one was riding slowly along the road. Her mother rose from the loom, and standing by the open window she watched the approaching figure with great interest. Then Queen Ute said:–

"That is no wandering harper, child, for see how nobly he sits his horse. It is some knight with tidings from a far country, or some king come hither to claim your brother's hospitality. But summon Hagen and question him concerning the stranger." So Kriemhild went out into the hall where Gunther and his vassals sat at the great table drinking and singing war-songs. Stepping softly to her uncle's side, she whispered that a stranger was approaching the castle, and begged him to look out and see if he knew who the rider might be.

Hagen was the oldest and most formidable warrior in all the land of Burgundy. He was tall and powerfully built, and gave the impression of great strength, in spite of his grey hairs. His face was dark and deeply furrowed, and the frown which he always wore made him look grim and stern, as indeed he was. He had never been known to care for anyone or to show the least regard for even his own sister Ute and her household. Only toward Gunther, his liege lord, did Hagen have perfect loyalty and a kind of doglike fidelity, which kept him ever at the king's side in the midst of the fiercest battles, and constant at his service at the court when Gunther needed his advice or support. He was famous, too, for his skill in statecraft, and in all matters of government was considered wiser than any of the king's other counsellors. He also added to this a wonderful knowledge of men and things, and could recount the deeds of famous heroes, all of whom he knew by name and lineage.

When Hagen came to the window at Kriemhild's request, he looked out for some moments in silence, then he said: "The youth whom you see approaching is Siegfried, the slayer of Fafnir, and owner of a famous hoard. It would be well for the king if he made this man his guest."

The queen hastened to send word to the porters to open the castle gates and invite the stranger to enter. Then she told the king that a noble prince had come to be his guest.

So Gunther and Hagen, followed by a retinue of knights, went to the great door of the palace and welcomed Siegfried to Burgundy. The young hero was surprised and pleased at such a cordial reception, and when the king urged him to remain with them some days, he gladly consented, for the castle with its gracious household seemed a pleasant resting-place after his days of wandering.

Many feasts were now given, and games were held in Siegfried's honour, to which all the princes of Burgundy were invited. The king would not allow him to speak of leaving them, and Siegfried was readily persuaded to stay yet longer, for the days passed quickly and happily at Gunther's court. The king became his friend and constant companion, and the beautiful Kriemhild often talked with him. Only Hagen kept aloof, grim, silent and distrustful.

Just before Siegfried's arrival, Gunther had become involved in a war with one of the neighbouring princes, and as the number of his forces was much inferior to that of the enemy, he feared defeat and the possible loss of his crown. Since the very beginning, fortune had been against him, and he grew daily more fearful lest it should end in the overthrow of his kingdom. Not wishing to risk another disastrous battle, Hagen went to the king one day and said: "Let us not allow Siegfried to sit idly here in the palace while we go to the battle-field. Bid him help us before it is too late."

"Nay, he is our guest," replied the king.

"What of that," cried Hagen, impatiently; "he has been here many days, and, as he holds himself your friend, your cause should be his also. We need help, and he alone is powerful enough to turn the tide of battle in our favour. He has a magic cloak called the Tarnkappe, which is of little use to him as he sits here in the palace. He also has the mighty Balmung, which was forged from the pieces of Odin's famous sword, and which should not be allowed to hang idle at his side. With Siegfried as an ally, no enemy can stand against us. Entreat him, therefore, before another day has passed."

So Gunther sought out Siegfried, and, after telling him of the plight of the Burgundians, begged him to aid them.

"Right willingly will I join you, my friend," said Siegfried. "There is nothing I would gladlier do than help your cause. I would have been at your side long since had not your gentle sister besought me not to trouble myself over the affairs of your kingdom, and assured me that your forces were more than a match for the enemy."

The next day Siegfried fought beside the king, and then victory followed victory for the disabled ranks of the Burgundians. The soldiers rallied under his leadership, and went boldly into the fight, while the enemy fell in great numbers beneath the terrible strokes of Balmung. A sudden panic came upon the hitherto victorious host, and they fled in terror before Gunther's pursuing army. This battle was followed by many others in which the Burgundians completely routed the enemy's forces, and their leader was obliged to sue for peace. So the war was ended, and the heroes returned to their homes to exchange the sword and shield for the milder pleasures of the palace.

Soon after this, Hagen came again to King Gunther and said: "This great victory has proved how strong an ally we have in Siegfried. It were well, therefore, to keep him with us, lest trouble arise again and we need his help. Let us bind him to our house by some close tie, and as no bond is closer than marriage, you must wed him to your sister Kriemhild, who already looks upon him with favour."

"But that cannot be, much as I desire it," answered Gunther, "for Siegfried will not wed with my sister, since his heart yearns for Brunhilde, and he is even now planning to seek her in Isenland."

"All this is true," answered the wily Hagen; "and while Siegfried longs for the shield-maiden, nothing can be done; but summon your mother hither, and bade her mix for him a draught of

forgetfulness. She is skilled in magic potions, and will give us such help as we need."

Gunther sent at once for Queen Ute and told her of Hagen's plan, to which she willingly offered her assistance; and that night when Siegfried returned from a journey to a neighbouring city, she offered him a cup into which she had put a magic drink which made him forget Brunhilde and his ride through the wall of fire. Then he turned more kindly eyes upon the beautiful Kriemhild, and before many days went by, he sought her hand in marriage of Gunther and the queen. Even to the unfriendly Hagen did he urge the acceptance of his suit, and the grim old warrior replied, "Gladly do we yield to you this flower of Burgundy; but to no other man would we have given her for all his prayers."

When it was known throughout the kingdom that such a powerful prince as Siegfried was going to ally himself with the house of Burgundy, there was great rejoicing among the people, for Siegfried had already made himself both feared and loved. The wedding festivities lasted several weeks, and many costly gifts were distributed by King Gunther among his vassals.

Yet in the midst of all the rejoicing, a strange feeling of uneasiness oppressed Siegfried, and he felt himself struggling with some memory that would not take shape in his mind. As his troubled looks seemed to worry the gentle Kriemhild, he tried to banish the haunting memory, and join in the merriment that attended his marriage.

Soon Hagen, who knew that Siegfried was the possessor of Andvari's hoard, caused it to be whispered about that the young hero had brought no gift to his bride, and that he lived, with empty hands, upon King Gunther's bounty. When this rumour reached Siegfried, he grew pale with angry pride; then, in the presence of all the court, he made a formal gift to Kriemhild of all his treasure, both the chests of gold which he had carried on his horse, and the great hoard which still lay in Fafnir's cave. In his resentment and wounded pride he forgot the curse which still rested upon it, and because of the drink which Queen Ute had given him, he forgot the ring that he had placed on Brunhilde's finger. Gunther and his people were delighted with the magnificence of the bridal gift, and even Hagen felt satisfied, for he knew nothing of the curse, and hoped sometime to induce Siegfried to have the hoard brought to Burgundy.

23

THE WOOING OF BRUNHILDE

$\int$iegfried's days passed happily at Gunther's court, and now that he had become the husband of the beautiful Kriemhild he desired nothing better than to spend his life beside her in the pleasant land of Burgundy. Ever since the day of his marriage all of his former life seemed to be shrouded in mist. He but dimly remembered the forging of Balmung and his fight with the dragon Fafnir, while the meeting with Brunhilde had, owing to the magic potion, passed wholly from his memory. He was very happy with the lovely and gentle Kriemhild, who had wedded him believing that she alone had won the young hero's heart, for her mother had spoken no word to her of the Valkyrie whom Siegfried loved, or of the draught which had been given to make him forget her. As for Siegfried, he was proud of being chosen above all the other suitors who came to win the hand of Gunther's sister; and he was sure that there lived upon the earth no maiden fairer than the peerless Kriemhild.

One day there came to the palace an old harper. His hair was white and his figure bent with age, but he could still play wonderful music, and sing bravely of the deeds of heroes. Many days and nights he sang in the great hall of the castle, and the listeners never wearied of his music. Sometimes he laid aside his harp and told strange tales of his wanderings; and one night as he sat before Siegfried and King Gunther at the feast, he spoke to them of a certain country called Isenland, where dwelt a beautiful maiden whom many kings and princes had sought to wed. "But," continued the old man, "she has never yet been won, for she is a warrior queen, and to those who seek her hand she proposes a trial of strength with the condition that he who loses in the contest must also lose his life. This has daunted many a suitor, for the fame of the maiden's strength has spread far and wide, yet there have been some brave men who have dared to try, and, failing, have forfeited their lives."

"But why is she willing to marry, if she has more than a man's strength, and can go to battle like any warrior?" asked Gunther.

"She does not wish to do so," replied the harper; "but it is written in the runes that she must wed. She is determined, however, to yield only to the hero whose strength can surpass her own, and therefore she demands that all suitors shall meet her in this contest."

"What is her name?" asked the king.

"It is Brunhilde," answered the old man, and at this Gunther looked fearfully at Siegfried, wondering if the name would bring back to him the memory of his ride through the fire and his meeting with the Valkyrie. But on Siegfried's face was a look of entire unconcern, and he smiled as the blood rushed into Gunther's cheeks, and cried:–

"Look now at the king's face, Sir Harper, and see how quickly you have found another victim for the warrior maiden. Methinks he is already eager to behold her beauty and win her for his queen. How is it, friend Gunther?"

"Even as you have said," replied the king, "for I would fain risk my life to gain this wonderful maiden."

Indeed, Gunther was so much in earnest in his wish, and so determined to journey to Isenland, that no advice from Hagen could turn him from his purpose, neither were the gentle pleadings of Kriemhild of any avail. He would have Brunhilde and no one else for his queen.

When it was settled that he should go to Isenland, Hagen came secretly to him and said: "If you are really bent upon going on this foolhardy journey, and desire to risk your life for a woman who is doubtless not worth the winning, take Siegfried with you. He has the sword Balmung with which to fight your battles, should you be beset with foes, and he has also the magic Tarnkappe which renders him invisible. This will help to bring you out of many unknown difficulties. Urge him, therefore, to go with you."

Gunther did as Hagen advised, but it needed no urging to obtain Siegfried's ready consent to accompany the king. He had grown somewhat weary of the quiet, uneventful life at the court, and longed for new adventures. The beautiful Kriemhild wept and besought him not to go into a far country, and on an undertaking

fraught with many dangers; but Siegfried only laughed at her fears, and bade her get his clothing and armour ready for the journey. To Gunther he said, "There is one thing you must do if you wish me to accompany you, and that is to give me your promise not to take any train of warriors with us, but to go alone with only Hagen and your brother Dankwart."

This seemed a very singular demand, and Hagen declared that the king should not listen to it; but Gunther trusted Siegfried's discretion, and was willing to be guided by his wishes, so he consented, and no one prepared for the voyage to Isenland save those whom Siegfried had chosen.

Kriemhild and her maidens spent many days making rich garments and embroidering costly robes, for she wished to have the warriors of Burgundy apparelled as became their rank. Queen Ute, also, brought out from her large chests many fine fabrics and rare jewels, and with threads of purest gold worked beautiful pieces of raiment, that Gunther and his friends might make a suitable appearance at the court of Brunhilde. But it troubled her that no retinue of lords was to be allowed to attend the king, as was customary when royalty travelled abroad; and she felt some resentment toward Siegfried for compelling the ruler of all Burgundy to go to a foreign court with no followers save three of his own kinsmen.

While Queen Ute and Kriemhild were busy at their needlework, the ship on which the king was to sail was made ready, and fitted up with all things which might be needed on the voyage. The most skilful rowers in the kingdom were placed at the oars, and at last the ship was launched and the sails set. There was much weeping at the departure of Gunther and his friends, and the watchers on the shore felt that they would never return from the journey. But the heroes themselves were eager for the voyage, and full of hope that their adventure would be successful – all but Hagen, who stood on the deck, grim-visaged and scornful, for he had no faith in this foolish undertaking, though he would have followed his king to the ends of the earth.

The voyage to Isenland was long, but no peril of wind or weather followed the ship, and no dangers of rocks and shoals marred the pleasure of the journey, or hindered the good ship's speed. When at last they came in sight of a rocky coast, and saw on the top of the cliffs a tall, fortressed castle with frowning towers, Hagen told them that they had now reached Isenland, and that before them was the palace of Brunhilde. It looked very forbidding, and Gunther began to doubt if, after all, this venture had been a wise one; but Siegfried was light-hearted as ever, and the gloomy towers brought him no anxiety or fears. As they were about to land he said to the king:–

"One thing further you must do if we wish to win in this undertaking. Tell everyone at Brunhilde's palace that I am your vassal, and have come hither at your command to attend you."

Gunther looked surprised at this demand, but he consented, and on the way to the castle Siegfried followed behind the king, as became a vassal in attendance on his lord.

From her chamber window the queen was looking down upon the knights as they rode toward the castle, and calling her maidens

to her she said: "Who are these strangers that have come to our gates? They seem of noble bearing, yet they have no attendants, so cannot be of royal blood. Let some one go to meet them, and inquire of their names, and why they have voyaged to Isenland, for in the harbour yonder I see a white-sailed ship."

One of the maidens went away at the queen's bidding, and soon returned breathless with excitement.

"It is Gunther, king of Burgundy, my lady," she cried, "and with him are his brother and uncle, and a noble youth named Siegfried. I hear that they have come to match strength with you in the games."

When Brunhilde learned that it was Siegfried who was at her castle gates, she trembled with delight and surprise; for *she* had been given no draught of forgetfulness, and she well remembered the brave youth who had ridden through the fire and wakened her from sleep. If he had come to win her, she hoped that his strength was equal to his valour, and that it would surpass her own. For the first time since Odin took away her shield, and with it the glory of being a Valkyrie, she felt glad that she was a mortal maiden.

Word was sent to the lords within the castle to let down the drawbridge, and welcome the strangers to Isenland. The queen also bade them give the guests the best which the palace afforded, and do everything which would make for their pleasure and comfort. When she herself was arrayed in her costliest robes, she descended to the great hall of the castle. There, seated upon a marble throne, and surrounded by her chosen warriors, she received the stranger knights in royal state.

To Gunther, who approached first, she offered her hand and bade him welcome. This courtesy she also extended to Dankwart and Hagen; but when Siegfried stood before her she rose, and, taking both his hands in hers, she said softly: "So you have come again to seek me, Sir Siegfried, but this time it is not through a circle of fire. It is long since we last met, but I have not forgotten you, nor have I lost the ring you placed upon my finger. There is no one whom Brunhilde would gladlier see within her halls."

Siegfried at first seemed bewildered at her words; then a troubled look passed over his face, and he rubbed his eyes as if awakening from sleep. He gazed long into the queen's face, murmuring, "Brunhilde – the Valkyrie – the wall of fire." Then all at once a mist was lifted from his eyes; he remembered his ride through the flames, the sleeping maiden, and all of the past which had been so long forgotten.

Brunhilde saw the change in his face, but she mistook its meaning. She thought that he had carelessly forgotten her, and was now trying to recall some memory of her. So her soft manner turned to hardness, for her pride was hurt, and maiden shame forbade her to show favours to one who could so easily forget her. During all his stay at the castle she kept aloof from Siegfried, and treated him with more coldness than she showed even to the grim-visaged Hagen.

As for Siegfried, he knew that something had happened which had blotted out the memory of Brunhilde during all the years he had been in Burgundy; and he knew also that if he could now choose his bride, it would be the haughty queen who treated him so scornfully.

But he was here as Gunther's friend and vassal, and to help Gunther win this maiden for his wife; so he laid aside his own regrets, and determined to do all in his power to further the king's suit.

Soon after the arrival of the Burgundians, a day was set for the contest between King Gunther and the warrior queen. At the appointed time they assembled in the courtyard of the palace, and Hagen had many misgivings when he saw five hundred armed knights standing about, whose faces betokened no good-will to the strangers. However, it was now too late to retreat, and he muttered to the king –

"We have truly come hither on a fool's errand; for whether you win or lose in this contest, we will never be allowed to leave this place alive."

At this Gunther only laughed and said: "Your grey hairs make you full of fears, O Hagen; and your age makes you blind to the beauty of this wonderful maiden, for whom a man might well risk his life. But fear not for me, as something tells me that I shall win."

And he went away, leaving Hagen to mutter curses on the whole mad adventure.

When Brunhilde appeared in the courtyard clad in her coat of mail, the four Burgundian warriors approached her, and Siegfried said, "My liege lord has come from far to match strength with you, O Brunhilde, and should he win in the contest, there is none who will give you allegiance as his queen more gladly than the humble and loyal vassal Siegfried."

To this Brunhilde answered coldly, "Does your lord know the conditions of the contest and the forfeit we demand, should he lose?"

"He does," replied Siegfried; "but nothing outweighs the chance of possessing Brunhilde for his queen."

"Then we accept the challenge," said the maiden, and, turning to one of her attendants she added, "Bring hither my armour, and let the games begin." The servants then brought her a golden helmet, a corselet of finely wrought silver, and a shield broad and heavy enough for the most powerful warrior. After arming herself with these, her spear was carried in on the shoulders of three strong men. It was very long, and of such tremendous weight that no arm but Brunhilde's had ever been known to lift it.

While these preparations were going on, the Burgundian heroes were watching with amazement, half mingled with fear, and Hagen muttered aloud, "Shall we stand idly by and see our king slain by a woman's hand?" But Siegfried whispered in Gunther's ear, "Take courage and we shall win, only show no sign of fear." Then he slipped out of the crowd and hurried down to the seashore where the ship lay at anchor. Here he hastily donned his Tarnkappe and the magic shield, and then went back, unseen, to the courtyard, where Gunther had already taken up his shield, and Brunhilde was poising her spear in the air ready to throw.

He took his stand close to the king's side and whispered, "Fear not, only do as I bid you."

Though he could see no one, Gunther knew that it was Siegfried who was beside him, so he took courage and grasped his shield more firmly.

The signal was given, and Brunhilde hurled her spear at Gunther's shield. The blow was a terrible one, and both Siegfried

and the king staggered beneath it. Borne down by the weight of the spear, and by the force with which it was thrown, Gunther would have been crushed under his shield had not Siegfried broken the force of the blow by placing himself in front of the king, while he held before him the magic shield which he had taken from Andvari's hoard. Then he quickly raised the king, and before the astonished spectators realized what had happened, he picked up the huge spear and sent it, apparently from Gunther's hand, back to Brunhilde. It sped with terrible swiftness, and struck her shield with a tremendous crash, carrying the warrior maiden to the ground. In a moment she recovered herself and rose, flushing with shame and anger. Going to where the king stood, she said –

"That was a noble blow, King Gunther, and I count myself fairly beaten at this first game, but you must also win in casting the stone and in leaping."

As she spoke, ten men came forward, carrying an immense stone upon their shoulders. This the maiden raised easily in her white arms, and swinging it once or twice above her head, she threw it to the farther end of the castle yard, some hundred yards away, and then leaped after it, landing just beside it.

The followers of Brunhilde shouted with delight, and every face showed pride in their wonderful queen; but Dankwart trembled with fear, and old Hagen bit his lip and cursed the day that had brought them to Isenland. At Gunther's side, however, was Siegfried, still whispering courage to the king, who could not see his friend, though he knew who it was that was winning the contest for him. Together they walked to where the great stone was lying, and Siegfried raised it from the ground, while it seemed to the spectators that it was lifted by the king's hand. Then he swung it above his head, and hurled it across the courtyard, where it landed far beyond the spot from which Brunhilde had first thrown it. Immediately he seized Gunther in his arms and sprang after the stone, reaching the very place where it lay half buried in the earth.

The warrior maiden could do naught but own herself beaten in all the games, and though her face showed disappointment and chagrin, she offered her hand to Gunther, saying:–

"We acknowledge ourselves defeated, my lord, and from henceforth Brunhilde is no longer her own master, but the wife and vassal of the king of Burgundy," and, turning to her knights and attendants, she bade them acknowledge Gunther as their rightful lord.

That night there was great feasting in the palace, though the hearts of the people of Isenland were heavy at the thought of losing their queen. She herself strove to appear happy and proud at becoming the wife of a hero whose strength surpassed her own; yet while she seemed to honour her liege lord, her heart longed for Siegfried, and she rued the day that had brought the Burgundians to Isenland.

24

HOW BRUNHILDE CAME TO BURGUNDY

o Brunhilde and the Lord of Burgundy were wedded, and, after many days spent in feasting and merriment, Gunther told his queen that they must prepare for the return voyage. It was some time since he and his friends had set out on their journey to Isenland, and he feared that if he stayed much longer at Brunhilde's palace, his own people would give them up for dead. Then he went secretly to Siegfried, and with a shamed, flushed face he said: "My friend and brother, I have come to ask your help in a strange matter. I cannot return to Burgundy with a wife who is my master, even as Brunhilde is now, for I shall become the laughing-stock of all my people. The queen of Isenland does not love me, and she treats me each day with more contempt. She does not scruple to insult me by making me the

victim of her great strength, which I am powerless to meet. Her might – which no other woman has ever equalled – depends on a wonderful girdle which she wears; and when I tried to wrest this from her, she tied me hand and foot and hung me on a nail in the chamber wall. Only by my promising never to trouble her again was I able to get release."

Siegfried felt sorry indeed for Gunther's plight, and he offered to try and subdue the warrior queen to her husband's will. So that night he assumed the form of Gunther, and wrestled with Brunhilde until he had taken from her the wonderful girdle in which lay all her unwomanly strength. He also took from her finger the serpent ring of Andvari which he himself had given her when they had talked together on the mountain. Brunhilde, being now quite ready to obey her lord, believing that he was truly her master by virtue of his superior strength, prepared for her departure from Isenland, and took with her as many of her own followers as Gunther would allow. He besought her not to overburden the good ship which had brought them thither with chests of raiment and household goods, since Queen Ute could amply provide all that Brunhilde might desire.

As to the wealth she had at her command, he bade her leave all that behind, for the rich lands of Burgundy yielded more than enough to satisfy the proudest heart. The queen therefore opened her chests full of gold and silver and divided them among her knights and among the poor of her kingdom. Her rich robes, and all the costly apparel she had worn, she gave to her maidens, and arranged to take with her only a small part of her possessions.

While preparations were being made for the departure of Brunhilde to the country of her liege lord and husband, Hagen was fuming uneasily at the long delay, and predicting all manner of misfortunes if they did not speedily leave Isenland. Gunther tried to allay his fears and said:–

"You are restless, Hagen, because you are old, and cannot share your lord's joy in having won this peerless maiden for his queen. There is really no cause for alarm, for the people here are friendly to us now that I am their acknowledged king. Besides, have we not Siegfried with us, and how can we fear any harm when he is here to protect us?"

"Yes, yes," answered Hagen, angrily, "to be sure we have Siegfried with us, but it is always Siegfried whom we have to lean on like a babe on its mother. Before he came among us, we ourselves were counted warriors worthy to be feared; but now it is always Siegfried who fights our battles, guides our ship, and brings us out of all our difficulties. It is Siegfried, too, who wins us a warrior maiden whom we would never have conquered alone, weak and nerveless men that we are. It is Siegfried, always Siegfried, and I hate his very name."

"Nay, now, good Hagen," said the king, soothingly, "these things should not provoke you to jealousy, but rather make you hold the youth in respect and honour. What would Burgundy do without Siegfried?"

"That is just it," retorted Hagen, bitterly. "Burgundy is naught except as she holds this foreign prince in her court. She boasts no warrior so valiant, no soldier so dear to her people, as this man

who came to us a stranger. Better far that he should return to his own country than to stay longer among us."

"Nay, nay," answered Gunther; "if Siegfried is so beloved by our people, it is a greater reason for his remaining with them." But Hagen shook his head, and muttered something which the king did not understand.

Everything was at last ready for Brunhilde's departure, and she bade a sorrowful farewell to all her household and to all the people of Isenland. Then she embarked on the white-sailed ship with the four Burgundian warriors. In a few days she was far out of sight of the land she loved, and was being borne toward a country unfamiliar and unwelcome. For even though she had been forced to own herself conquered in the games, Brunhilde had never been willing to become Gunther's wife, or to go with him to his home across the sea.

The voyage was quickly and pleasantly spent to all except the queen, who sat upon the deck, moody and silent, ignoring all Gunther's efforts to divert her. Siegfried felt happy at the thought of returning to the beautiful Kriemhild, though his heart was heavy with fear that the coming of Brunhilde to Burgundy would bring trouble and sorrow in its train. The evident dislike which the queen felt for King Gunther boded no good for the future to him or to his friends. Only toward Hagen did she show any kindness, and her overtures of friendship were, strange to say, very willingly met by the grim, reserved man. She would talk for hours with Hagen when no one else could get from her a moment's notice, and the grey-haired old warrior seemed ever ready to please and serve her.

At last the voyage was over, and the king was again in his own land and among his own people. Great rejoicing was made over his return, and feasts were held for many days in honour of the wonderful maiden who was now King Gunther's wife. But though everything was done for her pleasure, and many princes of the provinces of Burgundy came to pay homage to their queen, Brunhilde remained ever moody and silent. The gentle Kriemhild tried in vain to induce her to join in the feasting and merriment, but Brunhilde refused, almost angrily, and sat apart, brooding over her unhappy lot. After a time Gunther sought his mother, Queen Ute, and begged her to give Brunhilde some drink which would make her forget Isenland, and so be content to dwell with him. Queen Ute shook her head, and said sadly that she had nothing which could accomplish this for him.

The king went next to Hagen and said: "You have won Brunhilde's confidence, my uncle. Tell me, therefore, why the queen is silent and unhappy."

At this Hagen laughed mockingly and whispered: "Ask your noble friend Siegfried whom you love and trust so fully what it is that makes Brunhilde's heart so heavy with longing, and so full of bitterness. He can tell you far better than I." But shame and pride forbade Gunther to go again with his troubles to Siegfried, so he kept silent, and waited for time to cure the queen's grief.

Things went on in this way for some time, for nothing seemed to change the haughty queen, or soften her dislike for all of Gunther's household except Hagen. He remained her devoted follower, and her one confidant and friend. Toward the gentle

Kriemhild she showed both jealousy and aversion, though the sweet, friendly wife of Siegfried was at a loss to understand the reason for her sister-in-law's behaviour.

On his return to Burgundy, Siegfried had been unwise enough to tell Kriemhild of the stratagem by which he had won Brunhilde for the king, and how later he had wrestled with the mighty queen, and taken from her the magic girdle. He also gave Kriemhild the serpent ring which Brunhilde had prized more than all her possessions, but which she had yielded when – as she supposed – Gunther had outmatched her in strength. All this trickery Brunhilde did not as yet even suspect, so Kriemhild wondered at her ill-concealed hatred of the king.

One day Brunhilde and Kriemhild were walking together in the palace garden, and as they were about to enter the great feasting hall, Kriemhild, being a little in advance of the queen, was just crossing the doorway when Brunhilde called out angrily –

"Do you presume to enter before me, your queen? you who are the wife of a vassal?"

"I am no vassal," retorted Kriemhild, quickly, "for Siegfried owns allegiance neither to you nor to any other."

"That is a lie," cried Brunhilde, wrathfully, "for when Siegfried came to Isenland, he declared that Gunther was his liege lord, and himself a humble vassal."

"That was only to save your pride," answered Kriemhild, now dropping her angry tone, for she saw that the queen was in a towering rage.

"Gunther deceived me, then," stormed Brunhilde, furiously; then she added mockingly, "Since Siegfried is no vassal of the king's, I suppose he is a much greater and richer prince; that he is braver also, and stronger, and could outstrip the king in a contest of strength such as that in which Gunther won me for his wife."

"Even so," replied Kriemhild, "for it was really Siegfried who outdid you in the games, and not Gunther at all. It was Siegfried, too, who wrested from you the girdle and the ring, and he gave them to me as a trophy dearly won." As she said this, Kriemhild showed her two possessions and then passed quietly into the hall, while Brunhilde stood at the door too bewildered by her words to speak.

At length she realized the meaning of Kriemhild's speech. Full of anger and fearful suspicion, she sought out Hagen, and demanded that he should tell her all he knew of Siegfried's part in the contest. And Hagen told her how Siegfried had put on his Tarnkappe and stood before the king unseen; how he, and not Gunther, had flung the spear, and hurled the stone and made the wonderful leap; how it was Siegfried alone who had gained the victory, and he who should rightfully have won her.

Upon hearing this, Brunhilde wept in anger and sorrow, and said bitterly: "I might have known that none but Siegfried could claim the warrior queen for his bride. That fool and weakling, King Gunther, is no mate for Brunhilde, and never would he have called me wife had I not been tricked and deceived. He is a coward, and merits all the hatred and contempt I have shown him." Then

her anger grew fiercer than ever, and she swore vengeance upon those who had wronged her.

"Cherish not your wrath against the king," said Hagen, "for it is Siegfried who has brought this shame upon you. He has been a source of evil ever since he came among us, and he will yet be the king's bane; yea, and thine also. It were better that he died – and soon."

"He shall die," cried Brunhilde. "I will call Gunther hither and taunt him with his weakness and cowardice. Then if he is a man, he will avenge me of this insult which Kriemhild has put upon me."

So she summoned the king to her presence and poured forth the story of her wrongs, bidding him slay Siegfried if he ever hoped to merit anything but her hatred and contempt. The king listened to her words, but though he felt ashamed of the sorry part he had played, he would not give her the promise she desired, for he loved Siegfried, and could not find it in his heart to kill him, even to win Brunhilde's love.

Seeing that neither threats nor pleading would move the king to do what she desired, Hagen begged the queen to leave them, and give Gunther more time to make his decision. So Brunhilde went away, and when Hagen was sure that there was no danger of her returning, he came close to the king and whispered:–

"Blind fool that you are! Do you not see even yet why the queen has been unhappy ever since she came to Burgundy? She loves your friend Siegfried, and it is he whom she would fain call husband and lord!" Then he left the king alone, and Gunther sat for a long time thinking over what Hagen had said. He felt discouraged and sick at heart; for he knew that he was unable to solve the difficulties before him, or to avert the dreadful fate which seemed to be overshadowing him and all his household.

25

THE DEATH OF SIEGFRIED

Shortly after this Hagen came one day to the king, and said: "As long as Siegfried lives, there is naught that will appease the wrath of Brunhilde, or make her cease to weep. If you would have peace for yourself and would win the queen's love, it must be by Siegfried's death."

"But I cannot slay him, Hagen," answered Gunther, sadly; "he is my friend, and also my brother, and I cannot do such a treacherous thing."

"There is no need for you to perform the deed yourself. Only consent to having Siegfried killed, and another hand than yours will carry it out. It is useless to try and pacify the queen so long as Siegfried lives to arouse daily her jealous wrath. Consent, therefore, to his death," urged Hagen, "and I myself will slay him and take all the burden of the guilt upon my shoulders."

For many hours he talked with the king, working upon a weak will and unsteady purpose, and rousing in Gunther the jealous

fear that Siegfried would play him false. There seemed, indeed, only one way out of the difficulty, and at last Gunther consented to Hagen's wish and promised to aid him in carrying out his plans.

"If I cannot win Brunhilde's love except by Siegfried's death, then he had better die," cried the king; "for there is ever raging in my ears the queen's words: 'Never will I live to be mocked by Kriemhild. This thing must be ended by Siegfried's death, or my death, or yours. Would that I were again in Odin's hall – a shield-maiden starting for battle or returning with my weapons stained with red blood.' Do what you will then, my uncle, for I would lay down my life to win Brunhilde's love."

Having won over the king, Hagen went away, determined to avenge Brunhilde's wrongs and rid the kingdom of one whom he had long feared and hated. His plans were then quickly made. He remembered that he had often heard it whispered about the palace that some magic charm kept Siegfried from ever being wounded in battle, since no weapon had the power to harm him. So before he could carry out his plans, he must learn with certainty whether the report was true or false. There was but one person who would be likely to know this; and accordingly on a certain day when Siegfried had gone hunting with the king, Hagen went to Kriemhild, and seating himself beside her he inquired kindly if she were very happy as the wife of Siegfried.

Kriemhild looked surprised at this unexpected visit from her uncle, for he seldom took any notice of her; but she thought that he was prompted to a show of interest in her by his fondness for Siegfried. So she welcomed him gladly and answered his question in a way to settle all doubts concerning her happiness, had her uncle really felt any friendly interest. Hagen smiled at her reply, and said –

"Then what will you do if Siegfried is wounded in battle, and brought home dead upon his shield?"

"That cannot happen," answered Kriemhild, betrayed into further confidence by Hagen's seemingly affectionate concern.

"But such things do happen, even to the bravest warrior," persisted Hagen, "unless it be true, as I have sometimes heard, that Siegfried is invulnerable."

Not dreaming of his purpose in asking this question, Kriemhild proudly replied, "It is indeed true, and that is why I have no fears when my lord goes to battle."

"Was this great gift from Odin?" asked Hagen.

Now Kriemhild knew that Siegfried had forbidden her to speak of this matter to anyone, but she thought there could surely be no harm in revealing the secret to one so devoted and loyal as her uncle, so she told Hagen all about the slaying of Fafnir. She said also that Siegfried had been bathed in the dragon's blood, and that this was supposed to render him invulnerable.

"Was he completely covered by the stream of blood?" asked Hagen, with great interest.

"Yes," answered Kriemhild, "he was bathed from head to foot, except one small spot upon his shoulder, on which a leaf happened to fall."

"Are you not afraid that he may be struck in that place by a spear or arrow, and so meet his death?"

"It might indeed be so," said Kriemhild, "but I do not fear it."

"Still," persisted Hagen, "it would be well to have some one always near Siegfried in battle, to guard him against any death-blow, and since I alone know of his point of weakness, let me be the one to protect him. This service I shall be better able to render if you will sew a mark upon his coat over the exact spot on his shoulder where the leaf fell, so that when we are beset by enemies upon the road, or go forth to battle, I may keep beside him and shield him from a possible death blow."

Kriemhild was greatly moved by this evidence of loyalty in Hagen, and thanking him warmly for his devotion, she promised to sew upon Siegfried's coat some mark by which the vulnerable spot could be known. Then she hurried away to begin her task, not dreaming of Hagen's wicked purpose in obtaining her secret.

Some days later Hagen proposed that there should be a great hunt given in one of the neighbouring forests, and Gunther, who had promised to aid him in his plans, urged Siegfried to accompany them. Siegfried gladly consented, for he had greatly enjoyed this sport since his first coming to Burgundy, and had spent many a pleasant hour with Gunther and his knights in search of deer or fox, or the fierce wild boar. In all of these expeditions he had been foremost in the hunt, and had usually borne off the prize, both in the size and number of his game. His spear was sharp, and shone brightly as he rode along, mounted on the faithful Greyfel, and his aim was so quick and sure that his weapon never missed its mark, but went straight to the heart

of the beast he was pursuing. This superiority in the chase added much to Hagen's anger and jealousy, for as Siegfried had proved himself the greatest of warriors on the battle-field, so in the hunt he was the peer of all the knights of Burgundy.

A day was set for the great hunt, and a forest was chosen which was famous for the number and fierceness of its wild beasts. Then early one morning Gunther, Hagen and Siegfried set forth with their knights, in full expectation of having a profitable as well as exciting day. It was a beautiful morning in early spring, and the spirits of the hunting party rose high as they cantered out of the city gates and made their way toward the forest.

Siegfried rode ahead of the party, with Gunther and Hagen beside him. His suit was of royal purple, embroidered richly by Kriemhild's loving fingers, and his spear shone bright in the sunlight as he galloped along, light-hearted and unsuspicious of the black thoughts which were harboured in Hagen's wicked heart. He looked so brave and joyous, so beautiful as a youth and so gallant as a knight, that all the warriors in Gunther's train said among themselves that no one in Burgundy was fit to be compared to Siegfried.

These remarks soon came to Hagen's ears, and hardened him in his determination to slay this foreign prince whom all his own countrymen would so gladly make their king in place of the weak and unwarlike Gunther. He hid this feeling, however, and kept close to Siegfried's side, looking eagerly for the spot upon his shoulder where the loving but foolish Kriemhild had sewed the fatal mark.

The hunting party soon came to the edge of the forest, where they divided into three groups. Each leader took with him a party of followers, and they set out in different directions, with the agreement that when the sun was overhead they should meet at a well-known place where Gunther had arranged that their dinner was to be set out. Siegfried galloped away, and a greater part of the knights followed him. Hagen saw this and frowned darkly, but he said nothing, only waited for Siegfried to get out of sight. Then he whispered to the king:—

"Today is the day for our deed. This must be the last time that your friend Siegfried flaunts his superiority over the king."

Gunther trembled and answered weakly:—

"Must it be done, Hagen? Is there no other way to rid our kingdom of him?"

"No way but by his death," replied Hagen, firmly; then he added: "and do not you give way to foolish fancies, or my plans may fail. I have no womanish scruples, and Siegfried must die today."

Not wishing to have it appear that anything unusual was in preparation, Hagen ceased to confer with the king, but summoned his knights to the chase, and, putting spurs to their horses, they started through the forest. But something in the faces of the leaders made the men only half-hearted in their eagerness for the hunt, and a spirit of silence and gloom spread over the whole party.

They hunted all the morning, but their success was small, and when they finally drew up at the meeting-place, they found that they had very little game to boast of. The men had already come from the castle with great baskets of provisions, so the knights dismounted, and sat upon the grass to await the coming of Siegfried.

Soon they heard the loud blast of horns, and the joyous hallooing of men mingled with the barking and yelping of hounds; and in a moment Siegfried and his followers came in sight. They shouted merrily to their comrades, and galloped forward to join them, while those seated upon the ground looked with delight and surprise at the beasts which had been slain by Siegfried's skilful hand. There was a large black bear of the kind which was known to be so fierce that it was well-nigh impossible to kill or capture him. There was also a huge wild boar and three shaggy wolves, besides a great number of smaller animals, such as the fox and deer. The knights were all loud in their praises of Siegfried's wonderful skill, and he took their homage gladly, seeming wholly unconscious of Hagen's cruel face or Gunther's averted eyes.

Soon the midday feast was ready, and the men sat down to eat. Some of the game they had caught that morning was roasted and placed before them, and they ate almost greedily, for the sport had given them sufficient excuse for hunger. Presently Gunther said:–

"Is there no wine to accompany our meat? To eat without drinking is but a poor way to feast."

The attendant to whom he spoke answered:–

"There was no wine provided, my lord."

"How is that?" demanded the king, angrily.

"It was Prince Hagen's command," replied the servant, humbly, and at this Hagen interposed, saying:–

"Why should the king ask for wine when not a hundred rods away is a beautiful stream more clear and sparkling than the finest wine? Let us go there and quench our thirst."

"Very well," said Gunther; "and for my part, I am satisfied with the drink you offer. It remains for my guest to declare himself content."

At this Siegfried rose and exclaimed eagerly:–

"If that fear weighs upon you, let me prove how little you should cherish it. I will go first to the stream, and come and tell you how pure and sweet is its water."

"Let me show you the way, then," said Hagen, and as he and Siegfried moved away together, he asked hesitatingly:–

"Will you run a race with me, Sir Siegfried, to see which of us will reach the stream first? For though I am much older than you in years, I was accounted a famous runner in my time."

"Gladly," replied Siegfried; and they started off toward the stream. But although Hagen went with wonderful swiftness considering his years, he could not outrun the fleet-footed Siegfried, who reached the goal some minutes before Hagen came up.

"You are truly a swift runner, even now, friend Hagen," he cried gayly, "and I can easily believe your boast that you were once the most famous runner in the kingdom."

At this Hagen smiled and said –

"But what are we poor men, even the best of us, beside the noble Siegfried, who can outstrip all the warriors of Burgundy, no matter what the contest may be?"

"Nay, you are overzealous in your praise," laughed Siegfried, but he was pleased with Hagen's friendly words, for he did not detect the undertone of jealousy and anger. Then courteously he bade Hagen drink of the stream, but Hagen answered:–

"Do you drink first, and let me follow you, for though you would yield the courtesy to me because of my age, I would rather give precedence to you as the better runner. Drink, therefore, but first lay aside your armour, for the weight of it might throw you into the stream."

Siegfried, ever trustful and unsuspicious, threw off his coat of mail and laid his spear beside it, thus leaving unprotected the inner coat on which Kriemhild had sewed the fatal mark. Then he knelt upon the ground, and stooping over put his hand into the stream and prepared to raise the water to his lips. At this moment Hagen, with catlike swiftness, caught up Siegfried's shining spear, and, aiming it directly toward the mark, hurled it with all his force.

The weapon sank into the stooping body, and with a groan Siegfried rolled over upon the ground. As soon as he was able, he turned to see who had done this cowardly deed; and only when he saw Hagen fleeing in guilty haste, could he believe that the blow was dealt by one who so lately seemed his friend. Siegfried put his hand feebly to his shoulder, and when he found where the spear had struck, he knew that his wound was mortal. He made one great effort to rise, and gathering together all his strength, he drew out the spear and started in pursuit of Hagen.

The treacherous murderer had fled for protection to the king, and thither Siegfried followed him; but before he reached the

astonished and horror-stricken group who were watching his approach, the blood began to gush forth from his wound, and he sank helplessly to the ground. The whole company of knights knelt down beside him, weeping and lamenting over the loss of their leader. One of them raised the dying hero's head and placed it upon his knee, while others tried to stanch the blood from his wound. Siegfried, however, bade them cease their efforts, for his end had now come.

Then he turned to Hagen, and upbraided him for his cowardly deed, and for his treachery in obtaining the secret of his vulnerability from Kriemhild to use it in such a dastardly way. His strength was now almost exhausted, and his eyes began to close; but suddenly he roused again, and said to the trembling and terrified king:–

"Thou hast played a coward's part to thy friend who trusted thee, O Gunther, and some day thou wilt bitterly repent of having aided thine uncle in his wickedness. But for this I will not reproach thee, for thou art already sorrowing. One thing only I ask of thee, and do thou promise it, and make what amends thou canst. Take care of thy sister Kriemhild, and do not let Hagen's vengeance extend to her. Though thou hast proved an unworthy friend to me, yet I commend my wife to thy keeping. Wilt thou swear to protect and cherish her?"

"I swear it," replied Gunther, now weeping remorseful tears.

"Then see that thou play the man, nay, be for once the king, and keep thine oath to the dying."

As he finished these words, Siegfried sank back lifeless into the arms of the knight who supported him. All at once the clouds overhead grew fearfully dark, and the air seemed full of a strange, ominous stillness. The birds stopped their singing, and the forest was silent with the hush of night. The warriors stood weeping beside the body of their slain leader, but no one dared to speak. Slowly and sadly they raised Siegfried from the ground; and, placing him on their shoulders, bore him to the place where the faithful Greyfel was standing, patiently awaiting the coming of his master. One of the knights led the horse, while a solemn group of mourners followed, and not even the sternest old warrior among them felt ashamed of the tears he shed for the dead hero.

When the sorrowful procession reached the city gates, the news was quickly spread that Siegfried was slain, and by the hand of Hagen. There was great mourning throughout the city, and beneath the wail of sorrow was a muttered undertone of threats towards the man who could do such a cowardly and treacherous thing as to kill the friend who trusted him. But Hagen faced the people, calm and grim as ever, and said boldly:–

"Let all the guilt of this deed rest upon me, for it was by my hand that Siegfried died. Now there is but one lord of Burgundy, King Gunther, and no longer shall Brunhilde sit in tears, for the insult put upon her is avenged."

26

THE LAST OF THE HOARD

Though the news of the death of Siegfried had spread throughout the city, no one dared to bring the dreadful tidings to Kriemhild, who sat in her bower with her maidens, waiting her lord's return. The day was now far spent, and she began to wonder at his long delay, when the sound of some disturbance in the street reached her chamber windows, and she looked out to see what the unusual noise might be. At first she feared it was an outbreak of war, but the solemn procession which was wending its way toward the palace was not martial in its bearing, but full of the awful stillness of a funeral march. She saw that some one was being borne on the shoulders of the men – some one dead – and the others were his mourning followers. She wondered who it could be, and why they were bringing him to the palace.

Among the group of knights who formed the funeral train, she presently discerned the figures of Gunther and Hagen, and she began to tremble with fear and dread foreboding when she saw

that Siegfried was not with them. She strained her eyes to see if she could recognize the features of the dead, but she was too far away, and could not see; so she waited fearfully by the window, while the procession wound its way through the courtyard, and then into the great hall. Unable to bear the suspense any longer, she left the room and hurried down to meet her brother and learn tidings of Siegfried. But the moment she entered the hall, the faces of the men told her all she wished to know, and she did not need to inquire who the dead might be.

Everyone in the palace shared the grief of Siegfried's gentle wife, and all the city mourned with her in the loss of one so greatly beloved as the hero whom Hagen called a "stranger." As long as the first shock of Siegfried's tragic death engrossed all of Kriemhild's thought and feeling, she did not realize the part which Hagen had played in the event; but as the days went by and she had time to think of all that had gone before, she remembered how her uncle had traitorously obtained the secret of Siegfried's vulnerable spot from her, and how she herself had, at his request, sewed the fatal mark upon her husband's coat. She had heard that it was by Hagen's hand that Siegfried met his death, yet she could not believe him guilty of such a terrible deed. So one day she went weeping to Hagen, and asked him to tell her by whom Siegfried was slain.

"The story of such things is not for a woman's ears," replied Hagen, "and whether he died by my hand or another's is of small moment. It was the will of the Norns, who rule the life of every man, that he should die, and their decrees no one of us can change or avert."

When the day was set for the great funeral fires to be lit, all the princes of Burgundy came to attend the solemn festival, and sought to do homage to the dead hero by bringing rich gifts to be laid upon the funeral pyre. This imposing structure was erected in front of the palace, and on the appointed day the foremost lords of Gunther's household brought the body of Siegfried from the palace where it had lain in state, and placed it sorrowfully upon the funeral pyre. Beside him was laid his armour and his magic Tarnkappe, and last of all the famous sword Balmung. The king had ordered that Greyfel be carefully guarded for fear that if he were brought upon the scene, he would leap into the flames and perish with his master.

Around these things, which were sacred to the memory of Siegfried, the princes of Burgundy piled their most costly gifts, and everything was ready for the fires to be lit. But no one of Gunther's men could bear to place a torch to the wood, and a dreadful stillness fell over the whole assembly. At length Hagen came boldly forward and laid a burning brand to the pile of logs which formed the funeral pyre. In a moment the whole structure was ablaze, and the hungry flames leaped upward toward the sky.

Gunther stood by, trembling and fearful, lest Odin should send some terrible retribution upon the one who had slain his chosen hero. Kriemhild, weeping, hid her face in her hands, for she could not watch the dreadful fires. On the faces of all the watchers was reflected a great sorrow, for no prince of Burgundy was so dear to them as Siegfried, even though he came from a foreign land. Only

Hagen showed no grief or any sign of repentance for his deed, but stood by unmoved, like a grim, avenging god.

Then suddenly a figure appeared in their midst, wild and dishevelled, and seemingly mad with grief. It was Brunhilde, once a Valkyrie, come to claim her slain. Turning to the astonished group of mourners, she cried exultingly:–

"Look, you people of Burgundy, for the last time upon your queen whom you have ever seen fulfilling the common lot of mortal woman, and know that I was once a shield-maiden, one of Odin's Valkyries. I was condemned to eternal sleep by the great All-father, but was rescued by Siegfried, the hero who knows no fear. And here he lies who rode through the wall of fire to waken me, and who won me in the games by his godlike strength, though your cowardly King Gunther made false claim to me. Here lies Siegfried, the chosen hero of Odin and the true mate of Odin's warrior maiden. Therefore for him alone does Brunhilde own her love, and to him alone will she be wed. The Valkyrie yields only to the greatest hero." Saying this she leaped upon the funeral pyre, and in a moment had perished beside Siegfried in the flames.

And what of the ill-fated hoard upon which still rested Andvari's curse?

When the shock of the terrible events connected with Siegfried's death was over, and quiet was once more restored to Gunther's palace, Hagen came one day to the king and said:–

"You remember that Siegfried gave all of his treasure to Kriemhild on their wedding day, and although the hoard was never brought to Burgundy it still remains in the possession of your sister. Entreat her, therefore, to have it conveyed here; and, to accomplish your end more easily, tell her that she can honour Siegfried's memory by distributing his wealth among the poor. When we get the treasure into our hands, we will see, however, that nothing so foolish is done."

The weak-willed Gunther, always under the control of Hagen, accordingly sought Kriemhild and told her what great things could be done in honour of Siegfried, if only the treasure in the dragon's cave could be placed at her disposal. Kriemhild was not suspicious of her brother, for she did not know what part he had played in Siegfried's death, so she listened readily to his words, and said:–

"It shall be done even as you say, for naught can now bring me solace in my grief save some way to make the name of Siegfried dearer to the hearts of the people."

Then she handed Gunther the serpent ring which Siegfried had given her, and told him where to find the famous hoard in the cave of Glistenheath. She bade him keep the ring carefully, for Andvari might again have taken possession of the treasure, though he would yield it to the wearer of the ring.

The king took the ring from Kriemhild, and hastened with it to Hagen, who at once set to work to make preparations for conveying the hoard to Burgundy. In a few days a great number of wagons were fitted up, and with these a hundred men were despatched to gather all the treasure and bring it back to the palace. Although most of the men were Hagen's own followers, he could not trust them to go alone on this important mission,

so he placed Siegfried's ring upon his own finger and led the expedition himself.

The hoard was found securely stowed away in Fafnir's cave, and not a single piece of gold had been taken since Siegfried rode away after slaying the dragon. The dwarf Andvari still guarded the treasure which had once been his; but when Hagen showed the serpent ring, he allowed the stranger to enter the cave. He would have preferred to deliver the hoard to Siegfried himself, but the possession of the serpent ring made its wearer the rightful owner of all the treasure. So Andvari was obliged to admit Hagen's claim, and assist him in bearing away the gold.

Some days later, the company which had set out from Gunther's palace empty-handed came back laden with such wealth of gold and precious stones that all the riches of Burgundy seemed nothing in comparison. This great hoard was stored safely in Gunther's palace, and Kriemhild was very glad to find so much wealth at her disposal.

She became very lavish in her gifts, and eager to pour out all her riches, if only it brought added honour upon Siegfried's memory. No one who came to beg alms of her ever went away empty-handed, and the palace was always full of suppliants for her bounty. This extravagant giving went on for some time, until one day Hagen came to the king and said:–

"If your sister continues to distribute so much gold among the people, we will soon have them idle and rebellious, and then they will be useless to us in time of warfare. Bid her, therefore, to cease her giving."

But Gunther answered, "I have brought enough sorrow upon her through my evil deeds, and if this lavish giving can soften her grief, let her continue to dispose of her wealth as it pleases her, even though she should exhaust all the treasure that is in the hoard."

Hagen determined, however, that it must not be so, and seeing that he could get no help from the king, he planned to gain his end by other means. So he made every appearance of approving Kriemhild's lavish gifts, and in time prevailed upon her to give him access to the treasure, that he might help her in disposing of it. Then one dark night he gathered together a band of his own followers, and stole all that remained of the hoard. They carried it from the palace by a secret passage, and brought it down to the river, where Hagen sunk it many fathoms deep. Neither he nor anyone else could ever regain it, but at least it was out of Kriemhild's hands.

Thus was the hoard of Andvari, with its fateful curse, placed forever beyond the reach of men; but the charm and the mystery which hung around its very name still lingered through all the centuries that followed, and today the sailors upon the river Rhine are still looking for some glimpse of the sunken treasure.

27

THE PUNISHMENT OF LOKI

The curse which the dwarf Andvari had placed upon the hoard, and particularly upon the serpent ring which Loki had wrested from him, did not end with the sinking of the treasure in the river. Both Hagen and Kriemhild had been wearers of the ring, and evil soon fell upon them as it had upon Fafnir, Regin, Siegfried and Brunhilde. Some years after Siegfried's death, Kriemhild married Etzel, king of the Huns, and was slain by one of his knights. Before this, however, she herself had struck the blow that killed the treacherous and cruel Hagen. With the burial of Kriemhild, the ill-fated ring passed forever from the sight of men, and the curse of Andvari was never again visited upon its unfortunate possessors.

Any other of the gods than Loki would have regretted the greed which made him tear the serpent ring from Andvari's finger, and thus bring misfortune upon so many innocent people; but Loki did not care whether human lives were wrecked by his misdoing

any more than he felt one moment's remorse for having slain the shining Balder.

The gods had never forgiven Loki for this wicked deed, and they longed very much to drive him out of their beautiful city, which had never harboured any other evil thing. But Loki was Odin's brother, and they dared not punish him until the All-Wise One was ready to give his consent. Odin knew as well as they, that the slayer of Balder was not fit to live among the gods; but he waited for Loki to commit one more act of cruelty before he drove the offender out of Asgard. This occasion came, at last, sooner than Odin expected.

One day all the gods were invited to a feast in the halls of Aeger, the sea-king; and a bounteous supply of ale was brewed in the great kettle that Thor had brought from Hymer's castle. Thor was not present at the feast, for he had been obliged to go on a long journey; but Loki was there, looking sullen and angry. No one spoke to him, and he sat silent and alone, trying to appear indifferent to the hostile looks that were directed toward him.

The palace of the sea-god was very beautiful, with its walls and ceiling made of mother-of-pearl so delicately laid that the light filtered softly through it. On the floor was strewn the finest golden sand, and all the food was placed in opal-tinted sea-shells. The only thing that marred the beauty of the scene was Loki's ugly, wicked face.

As the meal progressed and the gods grew merry over their cups, they almost forgot the presence of the unwelcome guest; but Loki brooded in angry silence, waiting for some chance to wreak his ill-will upon the whole company. A servant stopped beside him to refill his horn with the foaming ale; and one of the gods, as he watched this, said to old Aeger: "Your servants have been well instructed. They are as careful to wait upon Loki as if he were an honoured guest." When Loki heard these words, he flew into a mad rage; and, seizing a knife that was lying on the table, he struck the unoffending servant dead.

At this wanton cruelty the gods sat speechless; but Odin rose, looking stern and awful in his wrath, and with a relentless voice he bade Loki be gone. "Never dare to tread our sacred halls again, nor pollute the pure air of Asgard with your presence," he cried. So terrible did Odin look that Loki slunk away out of the hall, and the gods returned again to their feasting. Soon a great noise was heard outside the hall, and all the servants came running in, looking very much frightened. Behind them walked Loki, who came boldly up to the table and dared Odin to send him out before he had spoken the words he had come back to say.

Then he began to talk to each one of the gods in turn, telling them of all the foolish or mean or wicked things they had ever done – ridiculing their mistakes, and laying bare all their faults in such a dishonest way that each small offence seemed an act of monstrous wickedness. Not content with trying to shame the heroes of Asgard, Loki began to speak slightingly of the goddesses; and attributed to them all the hateful things that his malicious imagination could invent. He was just telling some shameful lie about Sif when a rumbling of chariot wheels was heard outside, and in a moment Thor rushed into the hall brandishing his

hammer. He had heard Loki's last words, and he made straight for the slanderer, intending to crush him with one blow of Mjölner. Loki, however, quickly changed himself into a sea-serpent, and slid out of the room before Thor's vengeful hammer could descend upon his head.

Taking his own shape, he made his way to the mountains of the north, and there he built a hut with four doors, opening north, east, south and west, so that he could see anyone approaching and could easily make his escape. The hut was close beside a swift mountain stream, and here Loki spent many days in fishing – for there was little else to do to beguile the long hours. Remembering how easy it had been to catch Andvari after he had obtained the help of Ran, Loki made himself a net like the one which he had borrowed from the ocean queen. It took him a long time to weave the net; and one day, just as it was nearly finished, he saw two figures standing on the brow of the hill. He did not need a nearer view to tell him that the tall forms so clearly outlined against the sky were those of Thor and Odin. He knew that they had come to punish him for his many evil deeds; but he did not intend to be caught without making every possible effort to escape. So he threw the net which he was making into the fire, and, hurrying down to the stream, he quickly changed himself into a salmon.

When Odin and Thor reached the hut where they knew Loki had been in hiding, they found that he had escaped them. Then Thor by chance stumbled over the logs on the hearth, and, in doing so, he discovered the half-burnt net. Picking it up, he cried to Odin: "So this is what our crafty Loki has been doing to fill his idle hours. There must be some brook near by."

"Yes," replied Odin, "and that is where he has just gone. He has changed himself into a fish."

So the two gods went to the mountain stream, and there they saw a salmon lurking in the depths of a pool. Odin had already mended the burnt net so that it was serviceable, and he quickly threw it over the fish which was now darting here and there among the rocks. He did not catch the wily salmon, however, for it slid into a narrow opening between two stones. Then Odin cast again, and this time the fish gave a great leap over the net and darted up the stream. Determined that the tricky Loki should not outwit them, Odin and Thor followed the salmon a long distance until the stream finally narrowed into a tiny rivulet. The salmon now gave another leap into the air in a vain effort to escape the enclosing net which Odin threw over it. Then, finding itself caught, with incredible quickness it began to work its way through the meshes of the net, and would have slid out of the gods' hands had not Thor suddenly caught it by the tail. Since that time, so the story goes, all salmon have their tails pointed.

Odin now changed Loki into his proper form, and he and Thor dragged the wicked god to a cave in the mountain. Here they bound Loki hand and foot with iron chains, and fastened these firmly to the rock. Then Odin placed over his head a venomous serpent which dropped its poison upon the face of the fettered god, causing him great pain. So, chained and suffering, he lay there in the cave, unpitied by either gods or men. Only Sigyn, his

faithful wife, felt any sorrow for his pain, and she sat always beside him to catch the venom in a cup so that it should not fall on the captive's face. When she was obliged to turn away to empty the cup, the drops of poison fell upon Loki, and he shook and writhed so terribly in his agony that the whole earth trembled.

So Loki lay chained in the cave until the day when, according to the decree of the Norns, he was allowed to break his fetters and become the leader in that terrible battle which ushered in the last great day – Ragnarok, the Twilight of the Gods.

28

THE TWILIGHT OF THE GODS

The gods hoped that when Loki was bound fast, there would be peace in Asgard, and an end to mischief-making on the earth. Odin knew, however, that the time was almost at hand when the end of all things would come; and while gods and men rejoiced in the universal happiness, Odin's face was full of sadness. He had given to the earth and to Asgard a brief respite from trouble by chaining the wicked Loki to the rock, but he felt that the day of reckoning was near.

The first warning Odin had of the nearness of that day was when a sudden deadly cold spread over all the earth, and he knew it was the beginning of that long, long winter which had been foretold by the writing in the runes. So sharp and long-continued was the cold that it chilled the hearts of men, and even crept upward to touch the robes of those who dwelt in the eternal springtime of Asgard. Though all the earth shuddered under the winter's icy hand, people everywhere took comfort in saying, "It

will soon be over and then the warm days will come." But they waited day after day and week after week until the season came which should have been summer, but still the snow and frost and chill kept the world fast bound. Not a flower bloomed nor a tree budded nor any green thing appeared above the frozen ground. Yet the folk of Midgard still hoped on, and waited for the summer that never came. The terrible winter lasted for three years, and everywhere the dead were numbered by thousands. No food was to be had except what by chance had been stored away, for nothing could grow in the land where ice and snow lay always thick upon the ground. Knowing that they had but a short time to live, men fought and killed each other for the mere love of bloodshed, and no one tried to restrain the crime and wickedness that stalked unmolested through the streets. The gods looked down from Asgard at the desolation on the earth, and they sorrowed greatly to see men trying to drown their fears or buy forgetfulness in deeds of violence and brutish pleasure. Only the frost-giants rejoiced over the long destructive winter, for they had always wished to see the whole world wrapped in fog and cold like their own dreary Jötunheim. They turned their envious eyes toward Asgard, and waited in grim certainty that the rule of the gods was soon to end.

There was still some warmth in Asgard, for all of the sun's rays were turned toward the sacred city; but Odin knew that they had but a short time in which to enjoy this scant comfort. The two grey wolves that were ever pursuing Sol and Mani were fed, during the long winter, by a frost-giantess; and one dreadful day they rushed after the chariots of the sun and moon with such unlooked-for swiftness that they at last overtook the shining cars and devoured the charioteers. Soon a thick darkness spread over all the world, and when the last gleam of light faded from the sky, all the evil things that had lain hidden for fear of the gods, or that wished to live away from the light – all these came boldly forth from caves and dark forests and holes underground, for they knew that their time had come at last.

Then a terrible rending sound was heard as if the very foundations of the earth were being broken up. There was a rushing noise like the outpouring of all the seas, and a trampling as of a million feet. The Midgard serpent reared its horrid head above the waves, and then drew its huge coils from around the earth, creeping slowly from the sea to the land. The Fenris wolf broke his chains, and sprang with a fierce leap to the rock on the mountain where Loki lay bound. With the help of Fenrer, the fettered god tore himself free of his chains, and roamed over the earth with the great wolf at his side, gathering together all the hosts of evil that were eager to war against the gods.

From Jötunheim came an army of frost-giants ready to fight with their old enemy in a last great battle; and out of Muspelheim marched a troop of fire-giants under the leadership of Surter, who carried a flaming sword. Through a deep cleft in the earth Hel crept stealthily out of her silent halls; and behind her trooped thousands and thousands of dusky shapes that would never have dared to come up into the light of day. The Midgard serpent, pouring forth poison from his ever-open mouth, spread his great

length across the stricken land, and glided on to the plain called Vigrid where Loki had gathered together a vast and hideous array. A cry like the howling of wolves rose up from the plain, and it beat in the ears of those who were waiting behind the walls of Asgard. It was a cry full of hatred and defiance, and when the gods heard it they knew that the challenge could not go unanswered. Sadly – for each felt it was the end – they prepared themselves for battle; and, while they made ready, the frost-giants determined to avenge themselves by taking possession of Asgard. So, before Heimdall could sound his horn to warn the gods of the approaching enemy, they began to rush across the rainbow bridge that led to the coveted city. They came in such numbers and with such violence that Bifrost broke beneath the heavy tramp of feet, and the frost-giants were obliged to return to the plain Vigrid and wait for the coming battle.

The gods, with Odin at their head, marched bravely out of Asgard to meet the great host of evil things which had leagued together to destroy them. Then a terrible battle was fought, the like of which had never been seen on the earth before, nor ever will be again. Though the gods fought with the courage of despair, they knew that it was useless to contend with the fury and strength and numbers that were arrayed against them. One by one the shining heroes of Asgard fell beneath the attacks of the madly exultant foe, and even the mighty Mjölner was powerless to avert the doom which had been decreed by fate.

Thor struggled fiercely with the Midgard serpent, and though he killed it at last with his hammer, the terrible coils closed slowly about him and he was drowned in the flood of venom that poured out of the dying creature's mouth. Loki slew Heimdall; but not before the gods' faithful watchman had dealt the leader of the evil hosts a mortal blow. Odin engaged in a deadly combat with the Fenris wolf, and was at last torn to pieces by Fenrer's terrible teeth and claws. Seeing the greatest of the gods so brutally killed, Vidar, Odin's son, sprang upon the wolf, and with the strength born of madness and despair, struck the great brute dead. Surter, the fire giant, rushed quickly at Freyr, and destroyed the bright god with his flaming sword. Then he threw fire and flames over all the earth, and soon everything was consumed in the terrible conflagration that followed. Ygdrasil, the Tree of Life, withered up and was caught by the wildly leaping flames. The great tree burned like a dry twig; and when the last leaf fluttered feebly toward the encroaching fire, the high walls around Asgard fell with a crash to the ground, and let in the devouring flames. The stars dropped one by one into the sea, darkness reigned over all the world, and time itself seemed blotted out forever.

Then silence and the brooding night took possession of the universe, and this lasted many, many years; but in time a new heaven and a new earth emerged from the chaos that followed the destruction of Asgard. The sun shone again in the clear sky, and the moon and the stars once more shed their soft light on the earth. The flowers bloomed as gayly as before, and the fields were thick with ripening grain. Then, when the earth was ready for another race of men, a certain man and woman who had lain

all these years asleep in the depths of a cave, awoke. They looked with delight upon an earth made fresh and new, and to them and to their children it was given as an everlasting possession.